Snow Spell's Heartbreak

Book 5 of the Mari Fable Mysteries

Emily Fluke

Also by Emily Fluke

-THE MARI FABLE MYSTERIES

Death of a Fairy Tale

Kidnapping the Classics

The Pinocchio Project

A Grimm Haunting

Snow Spell's Heartbreak

Book 6 (releasing 2024)

-THE BEWITCHER'S BEACH PARANORMAL COZY MYSTERY SERIES

Magic, Movies, and Murder (releasing October 2023)

Summoning, Skating, and Skulls (releasing November 2023)

Book 3 (releasing December 2023)

-THE GARDEN PARTY GHOSTESS DUOLOGY

Garden Party Ghostess

Wedding Party Witness (releasing 2024)

-FOLKLORE FALLS ROMANCE RETELLINGS

Until Theft Do Us Part

Fake Dating's a Beast

"To all those who love fairy tales and keep the classics alive. You make magic real."

Prologue

Dear Journal,

Is it possible for pregnancy to kill me? Asking for a friend named me. The only two creatures on Earth with a gestation period as long as two years are elephants and Mari Rowan. Don't quote me on that, I'm not an animal expert. I'm not even a Mari expert—I thought mortality returned to me a fully non-magical state while it temporarily sealed the rift, but a nineteen-month pregnancy says otherwise.

On that note, the Brothers Grimm were wrong too. Fairy tales couldn't slip from Storyland into our world while the hood kept it fully sealed. Scarlet solved dozens of murders and crimes since then and not a single one resembled a fictional tale. We'd confirmed it, even revisiting the sight of the rift to be sure the seal still held. San Francisco's murders returned to crimes of passion and routine muggings rather than villainous plots.

Speaking of which, I needed to give birth so I could clear the fuzzy pregnancy distractions from my mind and return to work.

Don't get me wrong, I'm grateful for this baby. But hiding a two-year pregnancy from your boss and friends so they don't realize you're tainted by an eternal hood that you sacrificed to save the world from story villains... well, it gets exhausting. Not to mention the vomit.

Scarlet's sick of covering for me at Bay Side Media, but the good news is, I think I'll get answers soon. My wonderful, grumpy, but wonderful, husband found us a midwife who's willing to take me on as a patient. Or maybe she found him? I'm fuzzy on the details since Kai and I have been a little distant lately.

I can't help it that pregnancy makes me take over the entire bed.

Anyway, after months of doctors telling me I'm crazy, "There's no baby, blah, blah, blah," I'll finally get another ultrasound.

Because I know this baby is in there, and I think our child is the reason this summer is freezing cold. Or at least the reason I'm freezing cold.

Chapter One

"Death walks faster than the wind and never returns what he has taken."

— Hans Christian Andersen

Cold gel dripped down my bulbous belly, reminding me of the peanut butter and jelly I forgot to make for Wendy before sending her off to her last week of second grade. A lot of tasks and to-dos slipped my mind lately. I called it pregnancy brain, while Kai called it laziness.

I winced. Both the memory of his hurtful words and the pressure from the midwife's ultrasound wand triggered me. My gaze trailed past the woman's silver hair and landed on my husband's pinched face.

Kai perched on the edge of the living room chair between a coffee stain and a mark from when Wendy's crayon slipped off the coloring page. He kept his searing gaze fixed on the back of the woman's head. The midwife had positioned me on the couch and set up her portable ultrasound machine on the coffee table.

The Coffee Table of Evidence hadn't seen evidence in almost a year. Since the pregnancy, I'd taken on smaller cases at Bay Side

Media, opting to let Scarlet interview killers and deal with crime scenes. If I puked at the smell of Kai's cologne, pregnant me definitely couldn't handle the stench of a dead body.

The midwife, Christa, swirled the gel around my mountainous stomach and scanned her pale blue eyes over the small screen. The gel's chill couldn't compare to the odd, icy sensation that occasionally filled the inside of my stomach as though I'd just downed a whole Slurpee.

Christa squinted and nodded at the device, humming confirmation to herself. I craned my neck to glimpse the image projected from the ultrasound wand. Nothing but black and white static showed on the little device's glass screen and knots twisted my stomach.

Absentmindedly, I reached for the strings that secured the hood around my neck. My fingers found nothing, of course. The habit had stuck with me though the hood was long gone, sealed into the rift between worlds in Pioneer Park. Someday, maybe soon, it'd fray, weakening the veil between worlds and sending twisted tales into our world again—or so the Brothers Grimm had claimed.

I flexed my hand and rubbed my palm along my neck instead. My fingers found the chain of the small locket necklace Kai had given me as a gift last Christmas. He'd put a tiny photograph of Wendy on one side and left the other empty, ready for our second child's picture.

"Do you see the baby?" I asked, my voice squeaky and worried. Apparently, this woman believed in the unusual—whether, she referred to the impossible as supernatural, a miracle, or a curse, it didn't matter, I just wanted her to believe *me*. "I swear there's a foot in my ribcage." I tried to laugh, but Christa only frowned.

With a long sigh, she pulled back the wand and straightened from her hunched position on the edge of the couch cushion. She vigorously wiped the end of the wand and jammed it back into its plastic holder attached to the device.

"Yes," she finally said. "He's in there."

"He?" My eyes snapped to meet Kai's.

A grin—something I didn't see often on my husband anymore—spread across his face. Joyful wrinkles gathered at the corners of his lips and around his squinted eyes where hair had flopped into his face. Neither of us particularly cared about the gender of the child, just that they were healthy…and *real*.

"It's a boy?" he asked. Kai fiddled with the pocket watch locket I'd given him for Valentine's Day this past year. After the thoughtful necklace he'd bought for my Christmas present, I returned the favor with a historic-style silver pocket watch. One on side it told time the old-fashioned way while the opposite section of the locket held a small photo of our little family.

"Oh, you didn't know?" Christa said with a shrug. She was cold as ultrasound gel on a bare belly in the middle of an unseasonably chilly summer. *Ick.* "Yes, he's developing well. Strong little lad you've got in there."

"How—" Emotion choked up my voice. I coughed and tugged my loose sweater over my still-sticky stomach. "How far along am I?"

Christa raised her eyebrows and swept her cool gaze over me. "Two years, of course. Almost long enough for him to challenge me."

I scrunched up my nose. "Him, who?"

The midwife extended her finger, pointing at my belly as if magic might shoot from its tip. "The child. Your lad's a winter soul, and a powerful one at that."

She *knew*. She knew what I'd suspected. I blinked, half-expecting a red hood to materialize around her, though I knew it was impossible. But how did this midwife, this random woman, see the story aura around my son?

"What does that mean?" Kai asked, nearly shouting. He stood and balled his hands into fists. It looked like he'd readied for a fight, though Kai had never once raised his voice, much less punched a person, unless in self defense. Something about Christa set him on edge in a way I'd never seen before.

"He is magic." She swept her hand down the front of her body as if presenting a prize. "Like me."

Who in the wonderland was this woman? Clearly, or not-so-clearly considering I couldn't see the story aura anymore, she'd become a storybook character.

"Mari…" Kai shot his hand out to help me up. I took it and grunted my way to my feet.

A chill trickled up my spine. With the rift in the world sealed, no new fairy tale characters could slip into San Francisco and take over people's lives. Because of this, I didn't look for fictionally familiar characteristics in the people around me.

Until now.

Was magic how Christa saw the baby that other doctors didn't? I'd been so excited for answers that I didn't stop to consider the cost of getting them. Maybe a miracle-magic-believing midwife wasn't the solution to my invisible baby's problem.

Kai pulled me closer to him and away from Christa, putting his body between us like a shield, though the magical midwife made no move to threaten me.

"How did you find us?" he asked, slowly backing away.

I crooked my head at him and peered around his shoulder. Christa gathered the ultrasound device in her arms.

"What's going on?" I asked. Somewhere along the past two years of pregnancy and with the absence of the hood, I'd lost my story sight. Not only did the visual become fuzzy in my mind's eyes, but I'd fallen out of practice with the study of stories. And now, Kai and I switched places—he knew, or saw, something I didn't.

Christa clucked her tongue and stepped toward us. My belly iced over again, chilling me from the inside out. I'd have blamed the woman's cold stare for the feeling if it hadn't happened multiple times a day since I'd become pregnant.

Kai pushed back, knocking me onto my butt in the chair that sat kitty-corner to the couch. A huff escaped me as I landed, heavy belly and all, in the worn cushion.

"Hey! Kai," I breathed. I struggled to pull myself up around the basketball belly.

He wagged a stern finger at her. "Get away from me."

A puff of cloudy, white air swirled out from her harsh laugh. "Contrary to what you might have read, I'm not here for you."

My stomach swirled with sickness and my head with foggy confusion. Though the mist in my mind seemed to melt as I tried to pin which fairy tale character she matched.

Christa marched past him, gracefully squeezing between him and the Coffee Table of Magical Obstetrics. When she paused in front of our TV, her icy gaze landed on my stomach before her eyes flicked up to meet mine.

"Midwifery is only a side hobby. Something I'd picked up before I realized my true power, and a good thing too. I never expected an infant to threaten my reign."

I furrowed my brow and glanced between her and my seething husband. "Rain? It's cold enough to…" my voice trailed and my eyes dropped to the bookshelf that balanced our TV. Behind Christa's long, thin legs, were rows and rows of fairy tale books. The spine of one read *Hans Christian Andersen* in golden letters, just below the title was *The Snow Queen*.

I'd suspected as much, it was almost like a joke with both Kai and his sister, Gerda's names perfectly matching Andersen's tale. But after two years and only a few tiffs between Kai and I and losing the hood, I'd shelved the topic. Convincing your husband shards of glass from a troll's mirror forced him to see the ugly in everything, was no easy feat. Not only did my husband deny it on his grandma's grave, but digging for proof or answers regarding his storybook status only caused the rift between us to grow. The Grimm brothers had claimed that when the hood frayed and stories slipped through again, they'd be tainted and twisted, which meant I couldn't trust characters not to go totally rogue—including my husband.

My fragile heart couldn't handle it, not when dozens of doctors claimed I'd invented my pregnancy and imagined the nausea that came along with it. So, I'd dropped it and waited, crossing my fingers that his sister would somehow solve it for me.

"You're…" my voice trailed, I didn't have the energy to deal with a storybook threat beyond my husband's grumpy attitude.

It was all too much. Too much morning sickness. Too much at stake in our marriage. For once, I allowed myself to be…normal. But I'd dropped the ball, and now, the villain of the fairy tale stood in our living room, staring at my stomach with crystal blue eyes as though they'd shoot Elsa-level icicles through my flesh.

"A queen?" she finished for me, and a grin crinkled her cheeks. "Yes."

Kai scoffed.

I furrowed my brow and squinted at the ultrasound device in her arms. "How did you see our son when the screen was blank?"

"Get out!" Kai swept his arm toward the front door.

Christa only smiled, ignoring him. "You can't see your baby because—"

"Get. Out." My husband's voice dropped to a growl.

"Wait, I want to know." I hooked my finger through the belt loop on his jeans and yanked. Kai didn't so much as a stumble when I used him to pull myself up. I laid my hand on his arm and gently pushed it down. His muscles flexed beneath my touch, matching the tension in his jaw.

Despite his obvious discomfort, the quest for answers overwhelmed me. Christa didn't attack us, and she saw the baby that nobody else could. Either she played into my delusion, or I was right all along and I needed to know. I *had* to hear her say it.

"How? Is he...." I swallowed. I couldn't bring myself to say the word *real*.

"Because he's winter," she said it as if that explained everything.

Where was the child's body? How could I feel his little legs kicking the inside of my womb if he was a season? What fresh *Frozen*-singalong hell was this?

"And you don't like that," Kai added, still staring at her. He moved forward, but I held him back, using the pregnant-mama adrenaline that pumped through my veins to keep him in check.

It was just until she confirmed this child was a real, flesh-and-blood baby and not a figment of my imagination as all the doctors had said. Appointment after appointment I'd questioned my sanity while the morning sickness only grew worse and my stomach expanded. The doctors wrote it off as weight gain, especially when I'd admitted to working less than I once did.

"Explain," I demanded, feeling Kai's vibes of impatience and apprehension. Still, I wasn't willing to let her go, not yet.

Christa pursed her lips and arched an eyebrow at Kai before sucking in a breath. "Jack Frost can take many forms."

"Jack Frost…" my lips formed around the words but no sound came out.

"It seems he's already skilled enough to serve his mischief and hide when he doesn't want to be seen," she said. "You might have noticed your belly feeling chilly when he turns to frost."

"What do you want with him?" Kai asked.

Christa laughed and waved her hand. "Nothing!" Her weird smile wiped as fast as it'd come and she glared down her thin, upturned nose at my torso.

I rubbed my belly, feeling the solid pressure of the baby's skull pressed against my side. So much energy went into the development of the child that my mind struggled to connect dots. Exhaustion accompanied my pregnancy with Wendy, but it was nothing like the scrambled eggs that this magical, invisible—whatever he was—baby had turned my brain into. While my mind didn't keep up, emotions ran double.

A lump squeezed in my throat.

"Right, and I'm supposed to believe you're not the Snow Queen?" Kai said. "I didn't see it before but I knew something about you wasn't right."

"Winter is my domain," she snapped. "Muzzle the child or chain him in a basement. I don't care what you do but I'm telling you right now before he comes into this world, that he will not challenge me or you will all live to regret it."

Kai ripped from my hold before I could dig my fingers into his bicep.

Christa gaped at him as he grabbed a handful of her sweater's fluffy white fabric in his fist and shoved her toward the door.

The tall and elegant Snow Queen still walked with grace under the pressure of Kai's rough hand.

He swung the front door open and pushed her across the threshold without letting go.

"Unhand me, Little Kai," she spat. My husband only tightened his grip on the fabric until his knuckles matched the stark shade of her sweater.

Shaggy hair fell into Kai's eyes as he twisted his neck to glance back at me. "I'll escort her off the property. If my sister gets here before I'm back, tell her to wait before she goes to the hotel."

I'd forgotten Kai's family arrived in town today. His sister and mother hoped to get Kai's help to place their dad in a care home. Plus, I'd secretly hoped if Gerda and Kai reconciled their differences, it'd seal my husband's potential fairy tale struggle like the two friends in *The Snow Queen*.

"My boyfriend won't like the sight of this," Christa said, glaring at Kai. "He's coming to pick me up and if he sees you pushing me around, he'll explode."

"Good, he can pick you up and take you far away from us." He yanked her into the hallway and grabbed the door handle with his free hand.

I stepped forward, banging my toe against the hard leg of the armchair. "Kai—"

The door slammed shut. I could have ran after them, or waddled, and insisted that he 'unhand her,' but I didn't have the strength. I huffed and leaned my hip and one hand against the armchair.

For the first time in almost two years, I'd come face to face with a new storybook character. Or at least that I knew of, without the story sight. And, of course, she was a villain.

It'd been so long since I studied the classics, so many mornings of nauseous sickness, so many doctor's appointments, and so many disap-pointments when they denied what I knew to be real.

I swiped my cell phone from the corner of the coffee table and shot Scarlet a message. *My new midwife is a story villain. Need your help.* If she wasn't busy at work, she was with Carlos—but both could wait; I needed her story knowledge.

With a few waddling steps, I made it to the shelf beneath the TV where I popped a squat and pulled Hans Christian Andersen's fairy tale from between a copy of *Dracula* and Villeneuve's beastly novel.

I sank to the floor as I flipped through the pages, refreshing my lagged memory. Illustrations of the Snow Queen depicted her seated on an icy throne in the middle of a frozen lake. Behind her, a young boy stared at the ice's surface, looking pinched and sickly. My gaze glued to the boy's pained expression. I'd suspected my husband's role in this tale but had relied on the hope that the story world's influence had gone dormant with the rift sealed.

Was the hood peeling away? I knew it would happen, the Brothers Grimm—the gods of the story world—told me as much, but I wasn't ready. I'd only just received confirmation that this new child inside me existed.

And that Kai was…well, *Kai* from Andersen's imagination, come to life. Somehow the story aura must have slipped between the hood's seal between worlds.

My phone buzzed, and I blinked at the message from Scarlet.

Are you okay? Carlos is meeting me there, he says he hears shouting in your condo's complex.

My gaze blurred over the words, fixing on the digital clock. Did I lose track of time while staring at *The Snow Queen*'s illustrations? Kai had left with her almost half an hour ago.

I glanced at the picture of the chilled boy, facing his death on a frozen lake. I let the book fall from my lap.

"Shouting?" I said aloud. My mind shot to images of Christa attacking my husband, the same boy she kidnapped in her fairy tale.

A gasp died in my throat, and my stomach froze from the inside. A stark chill shot through me and I cupped my belly. Was my son turning to frost inside my womb? Could I trust the villainous woman my husband had dragged away?

Or was it a trick to get him alone? Did this follow Andersen's tale where the young boy becomes trapped in the queen's snowy realm, facing a frozen death?

"Kai," I breathed as I struggled to my feet. I didn't have the story sight, nor the hood to keep me immortal, and I couldn't even drink caffeine to get me going, but at least I had experience with the magic of the story world.

I had to keep my husband safe from the fairy tale that sucked him in before he froze under Christa's icy domain. Though the Kai in Andersen's story didn't die, saved instead, by Gerda, I didn't trust the cycle to play out correctly—not with the Grimm brothers' warning looming over me.

Like the wolf in my story as *Little Red Riding Hood*, the Snow Queen had fallen prey to her role and likely sought to carry out the story's plot for permanent immortality. Did that mean she'd risk freezing him to death to hurry the story along? If I waddled fast enough and got Kai away from her, nobody had to die. I made a mental note to speed-dial Detective Wilhelm.

"Nobody has to die," I repeated aloud. Arrested, maybe, if she'd taken Kai, but not dead.

My fingertips brushed the front door's handle. I grabbed it and twisted when a chilling scream split through the air.

The baby responded with a storm inside my womb, kicking and rolling over until my entire stomach froze.

Chapter Two

"When you have eliminated the impossible, whatever remains, however improbable, must be the truth."

— Arthur Conan Doyle

Though the air fell silent again, the scream rang in my ears. The heavy weight of my belly forced my feet in a wide-set position when I walked. It slowed me but I made it to the end of the outdoor hallway. At the top of the staircase, I leaned on the railing to catch my breath.

The mid-morning sun didn't shine, instead blocked by endless clouds that'd plagued San Francisco for too long now. A biting breeze nipped at my nose and my ears when the wind carried my chin-cropped hair from my face.

I peered over the railing to the concrete three stories down, searching for the source of the scream. Splayed on the sidewalk below, with her head twisted to the side, was the Snow Queen. A dark liquid spread across the gray concrete as it spilled from her skull. Her body lay in a contorted, unnatural position.

Ebenezer Scrooge.

A terrible sickness—far worse than any morning nausea or pregnancy pain—filled my stomach. Bile rose in my throat and I whipped my head away from the railing before it spewed three stories down and onto the body.

I was right all along. When with child, I couldn't handle the sight of death.

"Mari?" Scarlet's voice drew my head up.

I wiped vomit from my mouth with the sleeve of my sweater and looked over the railing again. But she wasn't down there. Scarlet bounded up the steps, gripping the railing on the staircase.

Had she seen what happened?

Movement from the parking lot caught my eye. I spied shaggy ash brown hair. My husband stood between two cars holding a shiny object in one hand and reaching out for something unseen with the other. I opened my mouth to call out to him but he vanished into the alley.

"Kai?" My voice died in my throat, too quiet—opposite of the woman who'd screamed. Only moments after she'd confirmed my baby's existence, my OBGYN now lay dead on the concrete. The sight of a lifeless body triggered my investigative instincts along with another reflex of gagging.

I swallowed bile and scanned the lot. Nobody else was around that I could see. The sound of a car's engine roared from the alley and I tried to make a note of it, imprinting the clues in my memory before distraction washed it all away.

Scar grabbed my shoulders and scanned me. "Are you okay?"

"I'm—" I shook my head and squinted at her. Scarlet never worried like this, even when I sacrificed the hood, and my mortality, she didn't fear for my life. Life was different for someone who'd lived for centuries. Not to mention she'd curated necessary deaths to save the fate of two worlds, too close together. Death, or the threat of it, didn't bother her. "I'm just nauseous," I said. "Did you see?"

Scarlet didn't so much as glance to where I pointed over the railing, but she nodded.

"Where did Kai go?" I asked, as I brushed her off and took the steps as fast as I could. By the time I made it down three flights of stairs, I couldn't breathe.

Carlos stood over the body, scratching at the back of his neck where his hair, the shade of an oak tree's trunk, had overgrown and curled. He craned his neck, twisting his head to look at me with a wrinkled expression. Though it'd been years since his flesh and bones turned back from wood and string, he still moved like a puppet with jerky gestures. It used to creep me out, but at least his nose didn't grow every time he lied.

He held a phone to his ear and gave the condo's address to someone on the other line.

"Where's Kai?" My mind was reeling as I tried to make sense of the chaos.

How had the Snow Queen died? Death wasn't possible for storybook characters whose fairy tale had yet to follow the plot. She'd only just found Kai. Did their thirty-minute exit from the condo count as her kidnapping and trying to freeze him? Maybe, but the story still wouldn't have sealed until the little girl in the tale found Kai.

I huffed as I took each step. Sciatic pain from the weight of a two-year pregnancy zapped across my back. At the bottom, I caught my breath and tried to rub away the pain in my spine.

Why in the wonderland had my husband run into the alley?

I kept my eyes away from Christa for fear of puking on Carlos, or Scarlet who stood behind me. Movement caught my eye from the shadow of the overhangs that housed the condo's parking spaces. A hulking figure jogged into view.

A thick, blonde-haired man that looked to be competing in a bodybuilding competition, ran toward us. Obvious pain twisted his face, where his eyebrows bunched and his mouth hung open. His massive, veiny leg muscles flexed as he dropped to his knees at the crime scene.

"Christa!" He cried out, but he didn't touch her body.

He's the boyfriend she mentioned. Had he made good on the threat Christa gave Kai? Did my husband run to protect himself? It didn't make sense; the boyfriend had only just arrived. Years of studying crime scenes told me to pay attention to the obvious suspect—the one who ran away, rather than toward the victim to help. Sickness curdled my stomach.

Like a baby deer on shaking legs, I stepped into the parking lot from the sidewalk. With one hand cupped beneath my belly, I jogged a few steps into the lot, glancing between cars for a glimpse of the alley.

"Kai?" I screamed.

Scarlet followed me, reaching for my hand. "Hey, what happened? Tell me."

"I don't know. Kai escorted the Snow Queen away from our condo. They were gone for longer than I realized and then I just heard a scream. Was–was it you who screamed?"

Deep crimson curls bounced around her face as she nodded. "No, but I heard a scream and almost joined in. Your text had me panicked and then I saw the bloody prints."

"Bloody prints?"

"Footprints." She pointed to the sidewalk where I'd avoided looking. A partial mark from the bottom of a shoe's pattern marked the concrete. The dark color of Christa's blood stained where her killer had walked away.

The zigzag pattern of the shoe's print looked especially sinister in the disturbing shade of red. Scarlet crouched to examine it more closely and worry struck me. Maybe it wasn't sinister, maybe it matched the shoe of someone trying to escape. Where in the wonderland was my husband?

"Kai!" I shouted into the parking lot. It was quiet in the complex at mid-morning on a weekday. Plus, the chill of constant, light snow had driven everyone to stay inside lately. I touched my temples with my fingertips and frowned.

The footprint could have been anyone's—it could have been Kai's. A panic attack loomed, rising in my chest to battle the pregnancy heart-burn. The only one losing in that scenario was me.

Dark spots dotted my vision. Throwing up breakfast left me weak and dizzy. I reached out for Scar to help me balance before I passed out in the middle of the parking lot.

"Was Christa a long-lost friend or something?" Scarlet wrinkled her brow. When had I told her the midwife's name?

Sirens echoed from somewhere in San Francisco. The familiar, big-city sound slowly grew louder and more piercing.

I leaned on her weight, clutching her arm with my hands. "No." I shook my head. "But she was definitely a storybook character and now she's dead before the story finished…" a choke caught in my throat. It wasn't possible, the story aura made everyone it landed on immortal until their story played out. There was no way Kai's little escort counted as the Snow Queen kidnapping him. That meant the plot wasn't finished and all the tale's characters should still be immortal.

"That's impossible," Scarlet said, but she didn't look surprised. The flat tone of her voice left me feeling prickly as we both trailed our gaze to the victim. "She couldn't have been a character."

"She was, trust me," I snapped, desperate for something concrete to cling to. "She even told us. Like all the other villains, she knew who she'd become."

"If that's true, then the rift isn't sealed by the hood."

"Or it changed how our world and the Storyland interact," I said.

"I don't believe it." Curls bounced into her face as she shook her head. "I hunted villains and dealt with the stories for hundreds of years. Nothing like this ever happened."

Were we really going to argue about this right now? I stopped scanning the lot to look at her with a frown. "Yeah, well, ever since I became the Keeper, nothing has been like what you knew. Christa was the Snow Queen and Kai was…well, Kai."

The twist of her pursed lips told me she didn't accept the truth. And why not?

Scarlet breathed a shaky sigh. "New characters are an impossibility," she spoke under her breath, but I caught the words.

It didn't matter what Scar believed. I knew Christa was the Snow Queen because she recognized winter—or rather, my son. All the pieces fell into place when Christa had identified my child's magic. The confirmation cleared nearly two years of stress and confusion. I knew, although I couldn't see the story aura anymore, that woman was the storybook character she claimed.

Was Kai the last to see her alive? If she could die, it meant Kai wasn't immortal either.

I knew how bad this looked. If I were the investigative journalist on this case, the first person I'd suspect was the man who'd shoved Christa from his house in an angry fit. But Kai was never like this, it was the story aura.

"Is it really impossible though?" I asked, scanning her face for a reaction. The strange, emotionless look from the Keeper she had been, returned. With her lips in a hard line and cheeks puckered to show the angles of her face, she looked harsh. It'd been years since I saw Scarlet as the hunter, as the killer she'd become to protect the world from story villains.

Her brow twitched, and she tore her eyes from the dead woman. She opened her mouth but only an exhale of white air came out and her eyes bugged, staring past me.

I spun around to follow her gaze.

My husband limped out from between a sedan and our SUV. A tire iron lagged in his grip, dragging against the concrete with an awful, ear-splitting scrape.

His chest heaved, and his lip was split. But the blood bubbling around his mouth wasn't what caught my eye. My gaze dropped along with my heart, crashing into the pit of my stomach where our son could turn it to frost if he wanted, apparently.

Dark, dried blood crusted Kai's running shoes.

My mind scrambled to remember *The Snow Queen*'s plot. The little boy in the story suffered some sort of spell that turned him unpleasant. But the story aura only landed on those who matched the characters, villains were already criminals with serial-killer tendencies. The kind, animal-loving ladies and gents became princes and princesses. Kai's only crime was his terrible dad jokes.

My husband drew in a sharp breath and stepped back, dropping into the shadow of the tall SUV.

"Kai?" I stepped forward.

"I didn't kill her…" he said, voice shaking. "I need you to know that."

"Of course," I said. When I brushed my fingers over his arm, he yanked away and dropped the tire iron. It clanged against the concrete.

"But I can't remember what happened. I found this weapon, and I picked it up before someone could attack me with it," he said with a shake of his head. "Or maybe I was mad. I was so mad at her, Mari." His brow creased and dark eyes swam with fear. "I was telling her to leave us alone. The next thing I knew, she was screaming. I know this looks bad…" He flinched further back, ready to run like a nervous rabbit.

My fingers closed around Kai's arm. With pregnancy strength and adrenaline, I kept him from stepping back again.

I glanced at the tire iron where blood was smeared on the crook. "What else happened?" I asked.

Cries from Christa's boyfriend faded from my attention and I blocked out the sound of approaching sirens. I gave Kai my full focus as I would any victim…or suspect. The lump in my throat grew thicker and threatened to choke me.

Shaggy hair fell into his face. He shook his head, while his gaze searched the ground. "I saw a figure and then the snowflakes. I followed the snowflakes."

Snowflakes? It wasn't the response I expected, and yet it made complete sense. It confirmed, once and for all, the fairy tale that had taken my husband.

"I couldn't stop staring at them. They were so beautiful…" his voice faded and his eyes glazed.

Though I was rusty on the stories, I knew this fit Andersen's tale. But with the queen dead, how would this story finish? Did this leave San Francisco to exist in an eternal winter? Would Kai forever be stuck under her spell?

A groan escaped me. No way would I let him get out of the chaos of raising another baby.

"Kai—"

"Did you see the snowflakes?" He lifted his free hand and touched something invisible in front of him. A crack split through my heart at the sight of him so deluded. I grit my teeth as confusion washed over his face. "They were here when I was with Christa but now they've disappeared."

"Mari?" Scarlet asked. Footsteps approached, and she peered between the vehicles. She raked her gaze over Kai, landing on the blood that stained his sneakers. "Detective Wilhelm just drove up."

Kai blinked, the glaze in his eyes partially cleared. He snapped his attention to Scarlet who remained emotionless, almost cold as she stared at my husband, the man who'd helped her get on her feet, like an adoptive father. But none of that warmth existed in her gaze now.

What in the wonderland was happening to my world? Like a storm, it went from calm to whiteout before I could so much as scribble a thought on a Post-It note.

Kai wasn't in the state of mind for an interview, especially not with his fingerprints on the murder weapon and the victim's blood on his shoes.

"I'll be back," he said, with clear eyes in a pointed look at me. In fact, his expression of concern made him look more like himself than he had in the past year. His warm hand slipped into mine for half a second while the other disappeared into his pocket and jingled the chain of the pocket watch locket. As if this were a first date or the day he'd proposed, hope and butterflies filled me at his touch.

He squeezed, and we stayed like that, holding hands, understanding one another. The moment didn't last. In a blink, the glazed look returned to his eyes and he let go.

At the sound of Detective Wilhelm's gruff voice, he turned. When he ducked out of the parking lot, disappearing from my sight, I didn't stop him.

Chapter Three

"What's done can't be undone."

— William Shakespeare

Like frost on a window in winter, ice built up around the outside of my stomach. Apparently, little Jack Frost didn't like that his daddy had just run away. And I didn't blame him.

While my belly had grown cold like this before, it was never this intense. Was the baby growing stronger, or did I only notice it more now that I knew?

I tore my gaze away from the empty alley between the condo and the apartment building next door. Kai had vanished only moments before Detective Wilhelm stomped up behind me.

"Rowan," he barked, breathlessly though he'd just walked a few steps from his car.

When I turned, his gaze dropped to the basketball I called my belly. His beady eyes bulged and his face paled all the way to his jowls.

I rubbed my stomach in a protective action, though the detective looked like my pregnancy somehow posed a threat to *him*. Sweat shined at his receding hairline. And while I'd gained weight and a giant belly, Detective Wilhelm lost his. Under the coat and gloves and scowl, he almost looked fit.

He cleared his throat and blinked rapidly before meeting my gaze. "Witnesses tell me you were one of the first on the scene. What do have for me?"

Wait, what? Detective Wilhelm passed up a perfectly good opportunity to go on a sexist rant about how I had feminine issues to deal with and needed to get out of his way. In all of wonderland, I'd never expected him to seek my counsel, *and* without examining the crime scene first.

I glanced at Scarlet who'd folded her arms and pursed her lips, clearly pissed that the detective didn't address her.

"I'm actually not working much right now—"

Detective Wilhelm waved his gloved hands to brush off my excuse. "I have a feeling you've got the details." His bushy brows furrowed as he squinted past me.

The murder weapon lay between parking spaces behind my slippered feet, complete with blood and my husband's fingerprints.

The mid-morning sun did its best to peer through the endless clouds. It cast a strange, yellow light on the side of the condo building, highlighting the third floor where I'd stood and looked down on Christa's dead body.

"The victim was my midwife," I explained, going into detail about how she'd left after the ultrasound. Of course, I left her claims about being the Snow Queen out of the story, as well as Kai's involvement.

Detective Wilhelm nodded while he took notes. His hand shook slightly as he gripped the pen. The cold drove even the toughest-acting men to wear cozy clothing. I half-expected Scarlet to tell the detective that he looked like a cute little kid with his gloves and scarf, but she wasn't herself, either. Scar's pinched gaze stared at Carlos who still stood where Christa had died.

I scanned the scene, my mind reeling after the confusing conversation with Kai. Did he know what had happened? Or had the vision of snowflakes distracted him? A shiver stole down my back and my stomach chilled from the inside out as if Jack wanted to remind me he was winter personified—not the queen of snow, the dead queen.

Crime scene investigators examined Christa and instructed her boyfriend to back away. Reese, the coroner, nodded acknowledgment to me across the parking lot. The man who'd become the Hunchback of Notre Dame had accepted the fate of his character's story, knowing all along who and what the story aura had turned him into.

Slowly but surely my investigator's mind took over as worry for Kai, and mixed feelings about the magical baby in my belly, shelved. The only way I could help either of my boys was to focus.

Was the Snow Queen's killer after Jack Frost too? Or was it a random occurrence? I had a million questions to write but the sticky notes were upstairs and I didn't want to miss if a clue revealed itself.

Who was on the scene first?

A familiar thought popped into my head as routine and practice with investigations pulled me in. My mind checked off each person in the parking lot, including my friends.

Carlos finally looked up, meeting Scarlet's gaze across the lot with a curt nod. I shifted my attention to her, but she snapped her head away. Though he stood beside the scene, Scar avoided him by marching to the other side of Christa's body where she stared at the bloodstain on the sidewalk.

Did they have a fight? Too many things happened at once. My midwife died, and as a storybook character. On top of that, my husband was gone. He'd fled the scene with blood on his shoes and snowflakes in his eyes.

Or glass.

It's the troll mirror, not him. Could the twisted tale have turned my best friend, husband, and confidant into a cold-blooded killer?

"No," I whispered to myself. Detective Wilhelm brushed past me and knelt over the tire iron.

I resisted the urge to check the alley again, in case Kai came jogging back with a smile on his face and no blood on his shoes. *Hey love, what's going on? I just had the most awesome run.* I imagined him in front of me with his once-normal behavior.

Those glimpses of the true man I married peeked through plenty over the past two years. But the grumpier side of him came out more often too—a side that revealed hints of the spell.

The movement of the detective's arms drew my gaze.

"Don't!" I said, as he reached for the weapon.

He craned his neck to look up at me, but he actually stopped. Detective Wilhelm listened to me. The world was definitely upside down.

He had every right to examine the murder weapon as he always did at a crime scene if it was present. I racked the recesses of my brain, the dark places where I imagined old filing cabinets that collected dust with stored information. What could I tell him to gain time for me to wipe my husband's fingerprints? And if I did, would I lose any chance of finding the actual killer whose prints should be alongside Kai's?

Or was this killer more cunning?

Christa's sudden murder felt more random than premeditated. Or had the killer known her schedule and followed her here?

"Rowan?" Detective Wilhelm interrupted my thoughts. "I asked you for a reason and you're just staring at me. Why shouldn't I examine this?"

"We don't know it's the murder weapon."

"True." He nodded, wiping at his leaky nose. It left a sheen of snot on his gloved finger.

True? I expected a *give it a rest, Rowan,* or maybe a sneer with *only lazy investigators don't consider every angle.*

In fact, it wasn't true at all. He should examine the tire iron and take it in for prints, right away.

"Well," he said as he stood. "I need to get the coroner's report. Do you think the victim fell?"

My gaze followed where he pointed at the condo's staircase.

"It looks as though she fell, doesn't it?" he said, again. "And who was at the top of the stairs with her?"

A lump caught in my throat as I felt his eyes fall on me. Was Detective Wilhelm really accusing me of murder… again?

Chapter Four

"The most difficult crime to track is the one which is purposeless."

— Arthur Conan Doyle

It wasn't the first time a cop told me not to leave town. Life as an investigative journalist threw me into plenty of precarious situations. But it wasn't until the story aura landed on me that the detective directly accused me of murder.

At least Detective Wilhelm let me sit down while he questioned me. The thoughtfulness still struck me as unusual, coming from him. As I waddled to the staircase, I purposely stepped on the bloody shoe print. I dragged my shoe against the concrete to smear the print in case Kai's shoes had a zigzag pattern on the sole.

Oddly enough, the detective didn't stop me from tampering with the evidence, though he clearly had his eyes on me the entire time. When had he become so calm? If I'd clumsily messed with blood at a crime scene in the past, he'd threaten to decapitate me.

I huffed as my butt hit the stone staircase steps. I squinted and raised my arm to block the sun as I looked up at the detective.

Detective Wilhelm tapped his pen against a clipboard, jotting down the details I shared. The patience in his voice unsettled me. Normally, he pushed for answers to solve cases as quickly as possible and feed his ego. Like Scarlet, he'd really matured as an investigator since I'd been gone.

With everything he asked, he ended each question with *am I right*? "Who did you see nearby? Nobody. Am I right? Did Christa behave nervously before she left? I doubt it. Am I right?"

When the detective moved on to question the distraught boyfriend, I caught the guy's name, Alistair. While he looked more like a Swedish bodybuilder, all jawline and veiny muscles with shiny blonde hair, he acted like a spoiled toddler. He rolled his eyes at the detective's questions and set his lips in a stubborn line the way Wendy looked when she refused to go to bed. After his tears dried and Christa's body bag was zipped, the guy whined at Detective Wilhelm for taking too long with the questions.

"Did you ever have any issues with your girlfriend?" Detective Wilhelm asked.

"What kind of question is that?" Alistair snapped. "We loved each other."

"So you've never had a fight?"

"I mean we were dating and neither of us are perfect. She was a little controlling, but I didn't care."

Detective Wilhelm nodded as he jotted something on his pad of legal paper. "If I check her phone messages, will I find out she expected you to be here?"

Alistar scoffed. "Yes, I already told you, I came here to pick her up."

"And you didn't see anyone, maybe running away?" Detective Wilhelm pointed to the alley where Kai had disappeared.

My heart skipped a beat. Did he know? *Impossible*. If he did, he'd be drilling me a lot harder and sending other officers to find my husband. Was the specificity of his question merely a coincidence?

I searched the cracked concrete on the sidewalk where tiny weeds sprouted despite the constant cold. After a deep breath, I calmed down and gathered my thoughts. As usual, I'd assign colors to clues and keep track of the mystery with my organizational skills.

My first list mirrored Detective Wilhelm's list. Who was physically close to Christa when she died? What had I seen and heard? Carlos, Kai, Scarlet, and the boyfriend were nearest. Any of them could have witnessed or been involved in the incident—based on facts, anyway.

A sickness twisted in my stomach at the thought of my friends as suspects. But if I looked at this as an investigator I had to include those in the immediate area before I considered motives.

In blue, the coolest color, I pictured my husband's name, only because I had to find how he fit into the scene. I'd never suspect him, even with the shards of glass from the troll mirror, or whatever had cursed him.

Yellow for the next closest... Carlos? He'd stood over the body, having arrived right after I did. Did that mean I needed to suspect Scarlet, too? She'd acted so strangely, overly worried.

Orange for Scar. It felt wrong to consider either of my friends but my experience as an investigative journalist told me not to rule anyone out. I craned my neck to where Scarlet and Carlos stood in the alley.

I reserved red for the boyfriend, though his initial shock at seeing Christa's body felt genuine. Maybe red was a shade too strong for Alistar.

None of the suspects fit the crime or lined up well with the victim. I blinked away my thoughts and scanned the parking lot. The coroner and crew had packed up and started rolling out.

What was I missing? My husband's innocence depended on my investigative skills, skills that'd gone stale. Hopefully, it was like riding a bike, though I'd definitely not be on any sports equipment soon.

None of my suspects made sense. I thought back to those first moments after running outside. *The parking lot was dead, pun intended.* I ran outside the moment I heard the scream—the scream that must have come from Christa herself.

Who had time to whack her and run? Only someone nearby, maybe with a getaway car...I recalled the sound of an engine. Scarlet didn't drive, but she was there, too fast, and Carlos too. And when had Alistar arrived? Was he there before and then came back to the scene of the crime? None of them were as clearly guilty as Kai, who'd left our house with his grip on the victim, then ran from the scene. But I refused to believe it, even with the strange curse on him.

"What am I not seeing?" I whispered.

Detective Wilhelm must have thought the same. He kept glancing at me as he wiped the sweat from his brow. If I didn't know better, I'd believe he wanted my help. Or maybe he truly suspected me, though the coroner had quickly cleared up Wilhelm's theory about the victim being pushed.

Christa had suffered blunt force trauma to the back of the head. Even an untrained eye could see that. Reese had confirmed she'd died from a blow to the skull.

Speak of the devil, the hunchbacked coroner returned to the scene, leaving his vehicle idling in the alley beside the detective's precariously parked sedan. White exhaust puffed from the van's tailpipe as it waited to haul the dead body away where she'd be examined for clues.

Clues were the next list I needed to create. Where had the tire iron come from?

Reese offered me a sad smile as he passed and approached Detective Wilhelm.

"I'm taking the body to the lab," Reese said, interrupting the boyfriend's rant about how he had places to go. Who worried about their schedule after their girlfriend just got murdered? I made a mental note to remember Alistair's complaints. "I'll call you if I get any clearer answers."

"Right." Detective Wilhelm nodded and wiped at his brow.

Reese cocked his head. "Are you okay, detective? With a red face and excessive sweating, I'm concerned you might be suffering a heart attack."

I craned my neck, twisting from my spot on the stairs to watch more closely. Reese was right. Detective Wilhelm looked ready to keel over, clutching his hand to his heart at any moment.

"I'm fine." Wilhelm barked, spittle flying from his mouth.

"Are you experiencing a sharp pain in your left arm?" Reese prodded. The coroner was nothing if not straightforward. He'd accepted his role in *The Hunchback of Notre Dame* with the same basic practicality despite the insanity of stories coming to life. It was how approached everything, even murder.

The detective glared at him, furrowing his brow. That was the Wilhelm I knew, grumpy, rude, and defensive. But then it vanished, fading with a strange smile on his face.

"You're right," he said. "Maybe it's best I sit down and get some rest."

At that, Reese and I exchanged shocked glances. If nothing else, at least, Detective Wilhelm was recognizing his limitations.

"After I talk to Mari again," he huffed. *Ah, there it is, the accusation.* "I have a feeling she's not telling me the whole truth about what she witnessed. These footprints lead across the lot where you were standing. Either they're yours, or someone else was here." His eyes bore into me, unblinking and darker than I remembered.

I couldn't argue his logic. The detective was good at what he did and Kai looked guilty…very guilty.

He didn't. My husband isn't a murderer.

Reese insisted on taking the detective's pulse before letting him interrogate me. With my luck, Detective Wilhelm would probably faint on top of me while accusing me of murdering my midwife.

And maybe that was best, for now. Until I figured out how to clear my husband's name, I could deal with an interrogation or two, maybe even another arrest, as long as Wendy stayed safe. If only we'd continued our day as planned. I imagined it as if it went well. First, we were supposed to have a quick appointment with the midwife, out to a husband and wife lunch date that we so desperately needed to close the distance between us, and then together to pick up Wendy from school.

"Mari!" A screeching voice broke through my thoughts.

Ash brown hair caught the corner of my eye but it wasn't Kai, rather, his twin sister. I'd completely forgotten his family came into town to find a care home for his aging father.

Pain twisted her soft features. I felt how she looked. Gerda mirrored her brother in many ways, the same shade of hair, same deep-set eyes, and they were both tall and lean. They even shared the same passionate personality. While Kai obsessed over history and nerdy historical facts, his sister adored psychology and studying the oddities of the human mind.

The frown on her face matched Kai's look of anger when Christa had threatened our baby. A scar above Gerda's mouth pulled her top lip up, making it appear fuller and as if lined with perfect, permanent makeup. Her repaired cleft lip was their only distinct facial difference other than her feminine, heart-shaped face. Dirty-blonde hair was pulled back from her face in a tight ponytail.

The yellow raincoat she wore fitted tightly against her torso. It rivaled her shiny red rain boots for attention. The boots clomped against the concrete as she picked up the pace and ran from the car with an Uber sticker in the window. I didn't have the energy to deal with *her* energy, but she deserved to know what was going on.

Gerda caught her breath and crouched in front of me as if I were a small child. She glanced at the detective and the coroner before holding my gaze. The glossy shine of her lip balm disappeared when she curled her lips inward in a concerned line.

While she usually spoke loud enough to make me cringe, she dropped her voice beneath normal-human level, a feat I never thought possible for her.

"Did he do it?" she asked, eyes wide.

A gasp caused me to cough as spit lodged in my throat.

"Did who do what?" I whispered when I caught my breath.

"Kai, is he guilty?"

My stomach went cold, icing enough to create frost on my flesh. I silently begged the baby to stop flexing his magic so I could properly process the shock I felt from Gerda's question. How in the wonderland?

"He texted me," she said. "I don't always keep my phone on unless I'm expecting a call so it was lucky I got his message. He said he's on the run for killing your nurse. So, did he?"

My heart stopped, and a sharp pain shot through my chest. It thumped, beating irregularly to make up for the momentary pause.

"How can you ask that…" my voice faded as another skipped beat tripped me up. I coughed and dropped my voice lower. "Kai would never—"

Gerda took my hands in hers, never letting her gaze waver. In a quiet voice she said, "Kai isn't in his right mind."

Chapter Five

"Words are easy, like the wind; faithful friends are hard to find."

— William Shakespeare

My sister-in-law was right, a pregnant woman shouldn't drink coffee. Also, my husband wasn't thinking clearly, but that didn't mean he'd killed our midwife. Steam swirled from the hot mug in my hand, carrying the delicious aroma of a dark roast to my nose. My whole body ached for a drop of caffeine and a warm beverage after sitting on the cold stone stairs in the middle of San Francisco's iciest day.

Not to mention the exhaustion of dealing with two rounds of Detective Wilhelm's interrogation tactics. He knew someone else was at the scene of the crime, and I didn't stop him from accusing me. At least it'd distract him while I figured out how to clear Kai from the situation.

I choked back a cry when Gerda took the coffee from me. She rambled about the psychology of worry and when a person finally snaps. It was entirely too easy for her to point out her brother's flaws. They'd had their differences, sure, but to accuse him of murder was going too far.

I tuned it out, focusing only on the sound of her stirring cream into the coffee. The spoon clinked against the porcelain cup that read *Best Dad in the Galaxy* beside a silhouette of Darth Vader. Tears pooled in my eyes at the sight of it and I nearly snatched it from her fingers.

It was Kai's mug.

My heart sat at the bottom of my stomach, getting a good icing from Jack Frost. I checked my phone again. After refreshing the app to locate Kai's phone for the one hundredth time in the past hour, it popped up with the same unsettling message, *no location found*. I swiped the app away and tapped into the message box to send another text. Even worse than being left on "read," it remained sent but undelivered with the dozens of other messages.

A shiver washed over my arms, prickling goosebumps along the way.

"I'm just saying, that's how people get when they're stress," Gerda said before taking a sip of her drink. I frowned at her.

Gerda continued her rant about how she noticed a so-called 'slow decline of her brother's mental sharpness' in the past year. Just because Kai was distracted with doctors insisting our baby didn't exist, and didn't throw himself into the study of the revolutionary war, or ancient Rome, like he loved to do, didn't mean he wasn't the sharpest tool in the hunter's kit.

When I broke my gaze from the cup, I met Scarlet's eyes across the condo. She sat in the chair where Kai had perched only hours ago and watched while Christa verified the existence of our second child. The wall behind her held a family picture of Kai, Wendy, and me wearing costumes at last year's trick-or-treating event in Pioneer Park. Though I stood next to my husband dressed as a giant version of Olaf from *Frozen*, it was the first time I'd felt normal and relaxed at that park in a long time. Wendy had insisted we wear costumes to match her little Anna outfit, with Kai as the snowman and me dressed in a fake fur coat and reindeer antlers.

Carlos bent down to say something in Scarlet's ear, pulling my attention from the Halloween memory. After nodding, she tucked a curl behind her ear and pursed her lips, never breaking our shared gaze.

The look on her face only made me want to grab the mug, but not to protect Kai's favorite cup. If Scar joined Gerda in accusing my innocent, dorky, maybe grumpy, husband, I'd waddle across the room and throw the coffee in her face. Once it was lukewarm, of course. I wasn't a psychopath, just really, really tired and angry and so confused. Here, Kai's friends and family surrounded me and I hadn't heard one defense for him yet.

Carlos, the guy we saved from certain puppethood didn't jump to stop Gerda's rant either. Instead, he folded his arms and nodded along as if Kai didn't deserve the benefit of the doubt. Kai had saved each one of us from various struggles throughout our lives, and here they'd turned on him in a witch hunt.

"How can you say that about him?" I interrupted, slamming my palms against the countertop. "How can you accuse your own brother of murder—"

"An accident," she interrupted. She didn't miss a beat, still stirring the coffee though the cream had blended. "I'm accusing him of an accident. Or an act of passion. People do far worse in the name of love. And Kai loved you and Wendy more than I've ever witnessed one person love another. You said so yourself, the midwife threatened your baby. That'd disturb any father."

She'd said it so matter-of-factly, so honest that when I wagged an accusatory finger in her face, heat rose to my cheeks. Breath escaped me as I dropped my hand and left it hanging limply at my side.

"Mari," Scarlet said as she stood. Carlos stepped aside so she could move between the chair and the coffee table. "You said Kai has been different lately."

"Yeah." I nodded. "A real *character*." I emphasized with a glance at Gerda. If she caught me talking about stories coming to life, she'd have me committed before I could say Ebenezer Scrooge.

"That's not possible," Scar said. A crease appeared between her brows then vanished in the blink of an eye. She shifted her gaze to Carlos who stepped up beside her. The flicker of uncertainty in her eyes was a familiar one. I'd seen the same look on murder witnesses who didn't want to confess the whole truth. It often meant they feared being found out by the very person they were meant to help the investigator locate. Maybe my job *was* like riding a bike.

I fell into the feeling of curiosity. Questioning and determination went hand-in-hand as an investigative journalist. Of course now, anger accompanied my curiosity, and I identified closer to the killing side of the metaphor than the cat side.

"You have no idea what's possible," I said. I folded my arms and my elbows rested on my belly, pressing against the spot where Jack Frost treated my sternum like a punching bag. "It's been a long time since you knew anything about what's *possible*."

Scarlet's mouth hung open as she stared at me. Carlos yanked up his button-down shirt's sleeves as if ready to join my baby in jabbing me.

"I think we're just emotional," he said. It wasn't me he shot glares at.

Scarlet nearly teared up—an action I'd rarely seen from the infamous villain hunter-turned TV-quoting investigative journalist. I glanced between them. What were these two hiding?

I'd finally gotten one question answered only to have dozens more piled on my shoulders.

A prickly feeling crawled up the back of my neck where a crick caused aches and pains since pregnancy had forced me to sleep on my side. Gerda's observant gaze suddenly entered my awareness. No doubt was she examining all of us through a psychologist's lens.

I swallowed and forced a smile.

"Kai didn't kill anyone, accidentally or otherwise," I said. "He saw someone else at the crime scene and I'll find out who it was. Then, our murder will be solved and nobody will have to accuse my husband of anything."

Gerda took a sip of her coffee then set it on the tall countertop that separated the small kitchen from the living room.

She cleared her throat and spoke softly. "I hope you know, I only want what is best for my big brother. He's lost right now and I intend to find him. I don't blame him for struggling with our father forgetting us and your marital troubles—"

"Marital troubles?" I scoffed.

Gerda raised her palms in mock surrender and maintained her soft voice. "Everybody is aware. It is normal and nothing to be ashamed of. You both have a lot on your plate with a child, and jobs, and another on the way."

I couldn't stand here and listen to Gerda analyze my life. Especially after she'd been distant from us for most of the time I knew Kai, only visiting on rare occasions. She was always too busy for her brother and her niece.

"Wendy," I blurted. I dug out my phone and realized the morning was long gone. The screen read half-past one in the afternoon and my heart skipped a beat.

"What?" Gerda asked.

"I'm late to pick up Wendy from school," I said. I waddled as fast as I could to the front door, snagging my purse off the coffee table on my way. "Hang out, drink coffee, whatever, I might not be back for a while."

As soon as the door slammed behind me, blocking my sight of three concerned and accusatory faces, I took a long breath of fresh air. It was cold enough to hurt my throat, but I didn't care. I'd just escaped a cage where my friends and family judged me at the same time as they called it helping.

The cool air cleared my mind, though I had to avert my eyes from the bottom of the staircase where Christa had died. I checked and double-checked my messages and the app to locate Kai's phone, but it yielded no results.

On the short walk to Wendy's elementary school, I took a quick detour. I swerved into the condo's parking lot and spied the tire iron on the ground behind our SUV.

I tried to crouch to pick it up but the shape of my stomach made it trickier than I expected. Before I toppled headfirst onto the concrete, I straightened and sighed. The baby felt heavier at times, especially when he didn't make my stomach cold, and now I knew why. Thanks to Christa, I understood that Jack Frost became frost, lightening the load of his human weight on my body. Then he'd return to being a regular baby when he didn't manifest as winter.

Right now, he wasn't doing me any favors, and I didn't have time for prenatal yoga in the parking lot. Instead, I kicked the tire iron under our car and hoped nobody would find it until I had time to return.

I continued to the school, arriving just after the bell rang. My daughter appeared at the gate among a sea of other elementary students. They wiggled, and skipped, swung their backpacks around and ran for their mothers…and fathers. I swallowed a lump in my throat and glanced at my phone again. *Where are you, Kai?*

Wendy hopped toward me and looped her fingers through mine. Her double-braids bounced against her pale, blue winter coat. The puffy, marshmallow jacket looked too small for her long, lanky arms. Finding winter clothes during the summer proved tricky.

The short walk toward home raised my heart rate, though we stopped often for Wendy to admire something in a shop's window or examine a small plant that'd broken through a crack in the sidewalk. As usual, she observed all that we passed—at least, all that interested her. The Starbucks display of new coffee mugs didn't catch her eye, and she barely noticed the cars that honked at one another in the crowded street.

When our condo's building came into view, my stomach knotted. I squeezed Wendy's hand and pivoted to the left. Something told me not to go home, not yet. After many evenings at work, I used to meet Kai at Pioneer Park to eat takeout and enjoy people-watching. Maybe just being there would help me feel closer to him.

"Want to go to the park?" I asked, averting my gaze from home where she'd see everyone's concerned expressions. Without explanation, Wendy would surely pick up on the situation. That'd put her in a precarious position regarding her father's whereabouts.

"Yeah!" she beamed. Wendy let go of my hand and skipped ahead.

Together, we hiked up the hill. While Wendy chatted about her classroom's upcoming talent show, I let Gerda's words roll off my back. I pictured the words crashing to the ground and rolling down the street. I knew Gerda cared for Kai and that this was her attempt to help, but I didn't have to love her harsh approach.

"Did you hear me?" Wendy asked.

I blinked and look at her walking in step beside me. We turned onto the pathway that led into Pioneer Park, passing a bench where Kai and I had shared many takeout meals in the past.

"Oh, say it again," I said, not willing to admit I wasn't listening to my daughter.

She grinned. A dimple sank the skin to the right of her curled lips. After Wendy nearly sacrificed herself to Storyland, she'd become more carefree. I'd told her that being strong sometimes looks like taking care of yourself. Over the past two years, while Kai succumbed to his story, Wendy thrived, absorbing the words I'd said to her at the rift.

We rounded the corner, and the full park came into view. To our right, a well-loved plastic play structure balanced over rubber ground. The pathway led to a center of concrete surrounded by streetlamps. More sidewalks branched off in several directions, leading to running trails through the enormous park's woods.

"I wanted to sing Elsa's song!" Wendy said. "But Jodi is already doing that. I'm not good at anything else." She sighed and let her backpack slip off her shoulders. It fell to the concrete with a flop.

I crouched and cupped my hand beneath my heavy stomach. Wendy didn't meet my gaze until I gently tugged on one of her braids.

"You're good at many things," I said with a smile.

The immediate downturn of her lips told me she did not agree. "Legos aren't a talent, Mommy." She referred to the buildings and situations she'd copy using the attachable blocks. Wendy spent hours recreating scenes she saw throughout her day or experiences she'd lived with Legos.

"What about singing a different song?"

Her eyebrows shot to her hairline. "Oh! Can I do the knife and apple trick?"

I cringed at the memory of when Kai had let Wendy practice tossing an apple into the air then catching it with the tip of a kitchen knife. He'd insisted it was perfectly safe since he had supervised the whole time. I'd let it happen since it taught Wendy quick reflexes and how to hold a knife in case she ever needed to defend herself in a pinch. We couldn't be too careful in a world where story villains will one day crossover again—at least, according to claims made by the Brothers Grimm. Supposedly, fictional character auras would return and the people on whom they'd land could become more powerful than ever.

"Um, maybe let's keep the apple trick for at-home talent shows."

Wendy's shoulders dropped again, and a whine escaped her. With that, she abandoned her backpack at my feet and dragged her feet over to the playground with two toddlers. Other than them, the park was empty, devoid of its usual runners, dog-walkers, and children of all ages. The cold had driven most to stay cooped up inside.

I smiled at the young mom who balanced her baby in one hand while breaking up a fight between her twin toddlers. Tiredly, she smiled back and lingered her gaze on my stomach. A spark of warmth ignited inside me as she recognized my pregnancy. The wounds of the doctors' denials were still fresh, though overwhelmed by fear for my husband's situation.

I straightened and tossed Wendy's backpack over one shoulder. While my daughter slumped on the seat of swing at the newly added swing set behind the play structure, I paced. The movement did my mind good while I continually refreshed the locating app. Over and over, it failed to identify Kai's whereabouts.

The messaging app whooshed as I sent off another text.

Please, get back to me. I trust you. Wendy, and I need you. And your son. We have to face the facts, you're a storybook character and it's time we figure out how to end your story.

It showed delivered and my heart skipped a beat. All the messages had switched from *sent* to *delivered* sometime between the school and the park. Had he just turned his phone back on?

I jammed my finger against the call button.

"Pick up," I whispered, still pacing at the edge of the playground. The cheerful greeting of his voicemail answered. I sighed and dropped my arm with the phone still gripped in my fingers.

What in the wonderland was he thinking? Running from Detective Wilhelm made sense, but going completely off the grid? I solved murders. Scarlet solved murders. We also both dealt with Storyland's magic and its influence on our world. How did running from the only two people who could help him make sense?

I stopped pacing, and I pressed the call button again. The lined trilled, ringing over and over. My heart sank as the voicemail answered.

I walked to a bench at the edge of the playground, the same one where Kai and I had cuddled and chowed down on orange chicken many times in the past. After a long breath, I tried again, this time typing out a shorter text message.

Kai, let me get rid of the snowflakes.

Did that count as a lie? I had no idea how to seal his story with the Snow Queen already dead.

A faint buzzing sound caught my attention between the screams of the fighting toddlers. I checked my phone's ring settings to see it was on full volume. The fact that the messages delivered now gave me a speck of hope.

I tapped the call button again and waited while it rang. The buzzing popped up, and I straightened, pulling my phone away from my ear. I huffed and leaned forward toward the source of the sound.

The buzzing sounded louder. Suddenly it stopped at the same time Kai's voicemail answered. My heartbeat picked up pace. I called him again and followed the sound of the buzzing.

Behind the park bench, in the soil beneath neatly trimmed bushes, a screen lit up with my face.

I gasped and dropped to my hands and knees. Once I reached under the bench and got my fingers wrapped around the phone, I pulled it out.

Quickly, and with shaking fingers, I tapped Kai's password to unlock the screen. My own messages popped up first after the call ended.

In the text box, but never sent, was a message meant for me.

I did it. I killed Christa. The other person who was there knows.

She witnessed the crime, but she knows I didn't mean to hurt anyone. She found me when I fled and she's going to help me. If I'm ever free of this again, I'll find you.

"I killed Christa," I whispered the message aloud to myself, feeling the words on my tongue. "You didn't, Kai. It's not you. You're not you."

Emotion suddenly overwhelmed me, too intense to swallow back. Tears slipped out and spilled over my cheeks as if floodgates had just been opened.

A thousand questions inundated me but my mind focused on only one thought. Gingerly, I touched my fingertips to the picture of us on the screen's background. The Kai in the photograph beamed at me with a generous grin, showing the dimple he shared with Wendy.

"I've failed you."

Chapter Six

"The whole world is a series of miracles, but we're so used to them we call them ordinary things."

— Hans Christian Andersen

Breath caught in my throat while the tears dried on my cheeks. He'd left me a breadcrumb, a clue, and a promise. What did he need to be free from? The accusation?

My mind reeled with the information. No way did Kai kill Christa. And who'd witnessed it? More importantly, how could this woman help him?

What he didn't say grabbed my focus the most. Even while fighting, Kai always ended a message with the same phrase—always. *You know I love you.*

Here, he'd left this note in a rush, no time for reassurance of love. Had the shards of the troll mirror fully transformed him? Could he only see the ugly in everyone he looked at? Whatever this witness claimed, she couldn't help him. Nobody except the Keeper of Stories could help him now.

First, I had to convince Kai, and everybody else, that he didn't commit murder.

I stood and spun around. "Wendy!"

My daughter's head popped up from staring at her dangling feet. The swing gently swayed back and forth but she wasn't pumping to enjoy a ride.

"We need to go home," I said.

She slid off the swing and dragged herself toward me, but stopped halfway. A toddler ran past her, nearly colliding into her side. Wendy snapped her gaze to the center of the park.

"Come on," I called out as I slung her backpack over one shoulder and pointed to the pathway that led out of the park.

Instead, Wendy walked the opposite direction. With her eyes fixed on the park's center, where icy wind scattered leaves across the open concrete, she moved in a daze.

"Wednesday?" I called her by her nickname. I yanked the backpack higher on my shoulder and followed her. "We need to go." My voice trailed off as I spied a hand-sized floating diamond shape in the middle of the park. It suspended in mid-air, right where the rift had once been.

Wendy walked up to it and stopped, staring. I tried to catch up, holding my stomach with one hand and pumping my other arm to help me waddle faster.

"Don't touch—"

A gust of icy wind interrupted me when an involuntary shiver overtook me. As if in response to the cold, the baby kicked. I stopped to brace for the freezing sensation coming from within. When Jack Frost chilled over, creating frost on the flesh of my belly, I no longer felt the painful wind and the heaviness of his weight lifted. Cold met cold and everything evened, if just for a moment.

I breathed easier and the biting cold on my nose and ears melted away.

The sudden burst of wind didn't seem to bother Wendy either, thanks to her thick marshmallow jacket. She stood her ground in the center of the park, too entranced by the floating diamond to care about the cold.

Wendy stretched out her hand. The diamond shape rippled with a multitude of colors—story aura. The closer I stepped, the clearer it became.

A scrap of red, heavy fabric had frayed and pulled away from the pulsing flesh of the living world…Storyland. I knew this would happen, the Brothers Grimm had warned me. I'd never be truly free of my fate as the Keeper of Stories.

Small fingers with chipped, glitter polish pinched the edge of the hood. I opened my mouth to tell Wendy to stop, *don't pull it,* but I was too late.

Wendy pinched the edge of the fabric and tugged, pulling it up to peek inside.

"It looks so different from before." She breathed.

Different? I squinted, unable to resist the curiosity. Plus, I needed to understand the changes the hood made to the story magic that returned to encroach on San Francisco.

Wendy was right. The rippling colors that beamed from the tear pulsed with an irregular rhythm, like an unhealthy heart.

For a moment, everything stopped, no colors, just plain gray as if clouds covered our sight of Storyland. Then the magic exploded like contents under pressure and a multitude of colors burst again. A beam of rainbow light cast from the diamond shape. Was this pulse pushing the story aura out into our world? Did the hood's magic only give Storyland a new lease on life rather than containing its effect on flesh and blood humans?

"It's Neverland," Wendy said, seeing a clear picture that I couldn't. "And Wonderland—I see Alice!"

"Careful," I said, stepping up. I cupped her small hand in mine to replace her hold on the hood with my unexplainably warm hand.

A thread pulled away and snagged on her fingernail. She stared at it, then shrugged.

"Okay, but I thought the characters were gone." Wendy looked up at me, ready for answers—answers that I didn't have. I wish I knew how it all worked. I wish I could explain it to her with confidence and tell her I knew the hood stopped the story aura from messing with people's lives.

Instead, I squeezed her hand and led her away from the fraying rift.

The only thing left to tell her was the truth.

"I don't know if that's the case anymore," I said. "But I do know we need to get out of the cold and find your Daddy before we worry about anything else."

At that, Wendy seemed to agree. She nodded and plucked the red thread from her fingernail, tucking it safely into her coat's pocket. For now, that was where the problem with the rift would stay. I didn't have the bandwidth to find my husband, solve a murder, grow a human life, *and* save the world.

Chapter Seven

"The fault…is not in our stars, but in ourselves."

— William Shakespeare

W hile I attempted to save my husband, lists saved me. Writing my priorities helped keep my head screwed on. For now, I tapped a reminder into my phone for reference after I found Kai and identified Christa's actual murderer.

Study the rift. Magic is irregular. How does this change how the story aura behaves?

I reread the note before clicking the side button to make the phone's screen go dark.

As we turned the corner to the staircase, a blast of wind greeted us. Wendy yanked the collar of her puffy jacket up over her nose. Inside of me, my son reacted too, meeting cold with cold. My stomach iced over and my body no longer felt the chill of the air.

Because nothing was ever easy, I expected a shift in what I understood about Storyland, the hood, and my role as the Keeper of Stories. Already, I'd barely scratched the surface of what was possible with the magic of fiction and imagination, and it was ready to change again. If I

47

got ahead of the game, and studied the changes before the rug pulled out from underneath me, I'd feel equipped to handle it. *Maybe.*

I let my gaze linger on the alley where my husband had disappeared. My heart beat in my throat. The rhythmic thump choked my voice. I couldn't speak when we turned the corner into the condo's complex and fiery, red curls came into view.

"Scarlet!" Wendy squealed. Shoulder-length braids bounced behind her as she skipped toward her pseudo-aunt. "You look different, Auntie Scar."

Scar stood, jolting straight from her crouched position beside the staircase. She stared at us with wide eyes from inside the circle of police tape. Four tall orange cones were posted around her in a square.

"Hey, hi, what's up?" she asked. Quickly, she tucked something into her back pocket and offered a flashing smile.

"What's that?" I nodded to her empty hands. "Did you find evidence?"

Instead of answering, Scarlet pushed her palm against the police tape and looked at Wendy. "You shall not pass," she said in a deep voice to emulate Gandalf. An awkward chuckle escaped her as she dipped under the tape and stepped away from the crime scene to give Wendy a hug.

I furrowed my brows and scanned her uncomfortable behavior. The way her eyes darted around but never met mine, the slight gnawing at the corner of her mouth. If I didn't know any better, we'd caught her in the act. The act of what?

"You didn't answer my question," I said.

"I'll race you upstairs," Scarlet said, spinning Wendy toward the steps. "But you get a head start."

Wendy giggled and darted for the staircase. Tapping footsteps joined the shuffle of her puffy jacket rubbing against itself as her arms swung back and forth.

"Knock so Gerda will let you in, Wednesday!" After I confirmed she heard me, I turned to Scarlet. "Did you find clues?" I arched to the balls of my feet and peered at the roped off area behind her. Nothing had changed. Blood still stained the sidewalk. In the chaos before, I hadn't noticed the amount of red that reached to the curb and stretched the stain into the gutter.

A queasiness came over me, worse than when I ate a meal Jack didn't agree with. My heart skipped a beat. Did I just call our son by the name of his winter personification? I blinked and focused on the person in front of me.

Scarlet kept her eyes on Wendy, refusing to meet my gaze.

"Scar, what's going on?" I asked.

She drew in a sharp breath and stepped away, keeping her back from my sight. "I'm just double-checking things."

"That's good," I said, moving closer to her. "What things?"

After a moment of silence, Scarlet forced an exhale through circled lips. Her eyes raked over the sidewalk, darting from the blood to her feet.

"Look, I saw Kai running away from Christa." Finally, she looked me straight in the eye. Now I wanted to turn away, but I held her gaze.

"Okay? He was there. We all know he was there, but the snowflakes distracted him—"

Curls spilled over her shoulder as she shook her head. "No, Mari, that's not possible."

"And Kai killing someone is?" I snapped. My blood boiled. *Screw the wind.* If the cold ever bothered me, it didn't have a chance in hell now. My entire body fired up, ready to melt the whole stupid city.

Scarlet raked her fingers through her hair, pulling the curls from her face. "He could have lost his temper, especially if he thought Christa threatened you or his children. What his sister said makes the most sense with what we know. We have to look at the facts. If this were any other murder, you'd—"

"This isn't any other murder! This case makes Kai look guilty. Kai, my husband, and the guy who has built every piece of furniture in your apartment, not to mention helped save your boyfriend's life." I slapped the top of my fist against my other palm in time with my words. "Kai. Is. A. Character."

Still, she refused to listen. Another shake of her head almost had me knocking it off her shoulders. *Thank you pregnancy strength.*

Though it was warranted, I didn't punch her and reined in my anger instead.

"What do you mean—" I copied her gesture, mirroring her shaking head.

"Storyland is sealed," she said with fake confidence. The quiver in her voice gave her away. I knew Scarlet almost as well as I knew myself—or so I thought. "There are no new characters, no aura, no magic. We only have the facts and the facts are that Kai was with Christa when she died. He has the answers, whether it's from witnessing her murder or…" her words trailed off.

"Or murdering her himself," I finished. I folded my arms, letting my elbows rest on my belly. "Right. Do you want to explain this sudden change in beliefs?"

Wind sent the police tape flapping and tossed my hair into my face. I plucked strands from where they stuck to the wetness of my lips. Unlike Scarlet, the icy gusts didn't leave my lips parched. I didn't shiver when another blast blew through the complex. Jack made sure of that, apparently, responding to each chill with more powerful magic of his own.

"You agreed with me before when I said Kai was…well, Kai from *The Snow Queen*," I said.

She clucked her tongue. "I never agreed. I listened because I was letting you vent. I thought it'd help you stop fighting."

I laughed without joy, and Jack felt my frustration. He kicked at my belly button and sent a few jabs to my ribcage. "This is rich. Real rich, Scar. You're the lady who lived hundreds of years thanks to story magic and suddenly you refuse to believe it. You know, you're starting to look pretty suspicious yourself." I let my arms drop and stepped toward her.

Scarlet ducked beneath the staircase and walked around the other side of the police tape to the curb.

"You were at the crime scene a little too quickly. You are the one who has actually killed people before—a lot of people!" My voice grew louder and pitched higher. "You tried to feed me to a wolf when we first met, with no remorse I might add. And yet, *you* want to pin this killing on Kai, a guy who scoops up spiders in a cup instead of smashing them."

Scarlet tripped off the curb as she backed away. With a quick grab of the heavy orange cones that kept the police tape in place, she righted herself before slamming her butt against the blacktop.

"What in the wonderland are you hiding?" I demanded, pulling out the same voice I used when I sent Wendy to a time-out.

"Nothing!" Her voice squeaked like a red-headed, or red-handed, mouse. *Mice don't have hands.* Before my easily distracted brain could go off on an internal tangent, I refocused.

"You have a reason to blame Kai and I think it's because you want to use him as a scapegoat."

"I don't even like goats," she said, pretending to misunderstand the phrase. "I'm more of a sheep girl really, they're so cute with their fluffy—"

"Scarlet!" I shouted.

She twitched and snapped her attention to me again.

"Come on." I tsked my tongue. "I'm married to a history teacher. That phrase has been around for centuries. Don't pull that crap with me. You have a secret."

"No."

A lie. Scarlet had lied to me a lot when we'd first met. I'd since come to learn all her tells to the extent that she refused to play poker with us during routine game nights.

"Someone lost their temper this morning, and it wasn't Kai." I pursed my lips and hugged myself tightly with my arms crossed in defense.

"Fine," she said, suddenly meeting anger with anger. "If you want to take the easy way out and blame the story aura and magic, let's just say *The Snow Queen* somehow slipped past the seal on the rift."

The frayed stitching popped into my mind. I'd already forgotten the diamond shaped exposure between worlds. I opened my mouth to fill her in on what Wendy and I had discovered, but she didn't stop ranting long enough for me to interject.

"If the story aura has descended on anyone, then I think it's you."

She jabbed a finger in my direction, pointing at me across the crime scene. Police tape, blood, and a million questions stood between us. I'd already lost Kai to snowflakes and supposed criminal activity, and I wasn't about to lose the only other person I truly trusted.

Scarlet side-stepped, moving toward the alley.

"Maybe Kai hasn't been grumpy at all," she said. "Maybe it's you that's unbearable. And I'm sure, you'll blame pregnancy but that's not a catch-all for rude behavior. If the story aura is back, then it's you, Mari, who has shards of glass in your eyes. The troll's mirror got to you."

"It's a devil," I said, correcting the character she referenced from Hans Christian Andersen's story.

"The devil disguised as a troll," she said, now standing at the edge of the complex as if ready to dart into the alley and toward the main street. "Get to know your fairy tales better if you're going to claim they're still real."

With that, Scarlet marched away, disappearing behind the building. She left me deflated and standing with my arms limp at my sides in front of a bloodstained sidewalk.

My heart pounded so hard with rage and fear and determination that I couldn't decipher the difference between my pulse and Jack's aggressive kicking.

I huffed. A swirl of mist escaped me.

For all I knew about how the story aura may have changed, Scarlet could be right. Maybe I was the little boy from *The Snow Queen.* Maybe Kai and I both were.

The dozens of things I didn't understand didn't waver my confidence. I knew, without a shadow of a doubt that my husband was innocent, my son was magic, and Scarlet had a secret. Could her past life have slipped through the cracks and caused her to attack another story villain? After centuries of hunting characters to seal their stories and contain the rampant and dangerous magic, it didn't seem far-fetched that she'd fall into her old ways. Did Carlos know? Was that why they'd both acted so strangely at the house this morning?

A million questions inundated me. Only one mattered.

"Who killed the Snow Queen?" I whispered it. My gaze glued to the ground where her body had been with her head twisted in the wrong direction. Once I answered that, the pieces would fall into place. It'd free Kai from suspicion which would let me tackle the mystery of the story aura's new behavior and how to rid it from him.

And maybe, it'd expose whatever Scarlet had to hide.

"Mommy?" A small voice cut into my thoughts.

I stepped out from beneath the staircase to see Wendy's braids dangling over the railing three stories above.

"I thought you went inside," I said as I hurried to the steps and waddled as fast as I could. The poor child looked frozen with red cheeks and the puffy jacket tugged up to her ears.

"It's locked," she said. "Aunt Gerda didn't answer."

I reached the top, wheezing and gasping for breath. After catching my breath, I followed her past the neighbor's condo and to our front door. The welcome mat covered the spot where I'd tried to trap Scarlet years ago. A cheeky saying decorated the brown bristles. I stepped on the words that read *definitely not a trapdoor* and unlocked the handle.

Wendy squeezed past my belly and dumped her backpack by the pile of shoes. Something crunched under my feet like a crumpled leaf.

I paused and looked down to see our extra key had been slid underneath the door with a note attached.

A grunt escape me as I crouched, cupping my belly. I pinched the note and straightened with another groan. Carefully, I smoothed out the crumpled sticky note and scanned the message. The handwriting was orderly, though the ink had smudged as if written in a hurry.

I'm worried about Kai. I have a feeling I can find him, so I'm going to hunt him down. If I find him, I'll call—Gerda.

Chapter Eight

"It is a capital mistake to theorize before one has data."

— Arthur Conan Doyle

The note weighed heavy in my hoodie's pocket—Kai's hoodie, actually. I'd stolen a comfortable, green pullover sweatshirt from his side of the closet. Lately, most of my clothes didn't fit, not without exposing the bottom of my stomach.

I folded and unfolded Gerda's note inside the large front pocket. Of course, Gerda didn't simply send me a text message. She always insisted on doing things differently and preferred to use her phone as little as possible.

After quietly closing Wendy's door, I snagged my phone from the kitchen counter. I pressed it to my ear but only got the same response as the first five times I called her. The other line didn't so much as ring, but answered with her voicemail immediately. Gerda's phone was off —not unusual for her, but horrible for my blood pressure. It spiked when the sound of her voicemail confirmed I had no way to contact her.

"I guess we're in a race now," I mumbled. I needed to find the murderer before Gerda found Kai and turned him over to the police.

For now, it was impossible to search the crime scene or interview suspects. I couldn't leave Wendy to pay Christa's boyfriend a visit. Even the parking lot was too far for me to stray from home with Wendy alone. My heart thumped in my ears, the only sound other than Wendy's soft snores from behind her door.

I leaned my hip against the kitchen counter and took a long breath, trying to slow my pulse. The thought of Detective Wilhelm interrogating Kai left me dizzy. I didn't want to imagine the detective's reaction to Kai seeing snowflakes inside the interview room at the station. Would he call Christa the Snow Queen in front of Detective Wilhelm? Or would he wrongly confess that he'd killed her?

The thoughts only heightened my anxiety. My heart thudded, occasionally skipping beats like the irregular pulse of the rift's living pressure.

"Stress isn't good for the baby," I muttered as I tried to take cleansing breaths. It was a repeat of the words my OBGYN told me eight years ago when I was pregnant for the first time.

I busied myself by wrapping the leftovers from our freezer meal in a plastic container. My heart pounded harder, as if cleaning the kitchen was akin to running from a wolf. Vigorously, I scrubbed at spills on the counter, using all of my strength to focus on the hardened spot of spaghetti sauce.

No amount of cleaning slowed my pulse. I couldn't wait around when I had a hundred questions I needed answered.

I slapped the wet washcloth against the counter and abandoned the spaghetti sauce stain. The couch sank under the weight of both Jack and me after I made my way into the living room. I peeled two sticky notes off of each colored block and arranged them in rows on the coffee table.

"Who has a motive?"

Scarlet: to kill a villain. Did Han Christian Andersen's Snow Queen fill that role or did her character count as morally gray? Either way, my accusation against my best friend didn't make sense. Of course, her denial of Storyland's magic didn't either. She had a secret, and only five percent of me believed it involved Christa's murder.

Carlos: no motive. Absolutely nothing.

I sighed.

"I guess that leaves the boyfriend." I tapped the pen against the table. "Seems too obvious."

Besides, Alistair's reactions had looked as genuine as grief could get. And I'd witnessed him walking from his car in the condo's parking lot. So whose car had I heard in the alley?

I scribbled the names of the people who'd driven to the scene of the crime but that didn't make sense either. The killer had likely sped off.

"I need more information," I said as I peeled the sticky notes off the table and stacked them into a pile. I couldn't organize my way out of this one and I wouldn't let any more time pass.

It took all of my strength to push off the sunken cushion and carry Jack and myself to the front door where I slipped on sneakers. The backs of the shoes smashed beneath my heels but I didn't care enough to bend around my belly and fix it.

As soon as I opened the door, my stomach iced over and the weight of my son lifted. A chilly breeze swept through the open hallway but Jack's magic seemed to protect me from it. I rapped my knuckles against Tala's front door, hoping it wasn't too late to bother her.

Footsteps approached the door from the other side but she didn't open it.

"It's Mari, Tala," I exclaimed.

The knob twisted, and she pulled it open. "I was so relieved to hear your voice. Can't be too careful after another murder around here."

I nodded. "How is Mr. Geppetto doing with it?" Another violent death on the premises had likely triggered the memory of his adult daughter's murder right in this very hallway not even a decade ago.

Tala rubbed the soft, wrinkled skin at the edge of her eyes with her fingertips. "Not the greatest. But wedding preparations have been a great distraction for him." A sparkle gleamed in her eye. Tala's delight at their engagement shined through our serious conversation.

"Can I bother you to babysit while I examine the crime scene?" I nodded toward our condo. "Wendy's asleep and Kai is..." A lump in my throat made the rest of the sentence impossible to say.

"No bother," she said. Tala pulled the door shut behind her and patted my forearm. "I hope you find who did it."

At my welcome mat, I thanked her and turned toward the staircase. "Mari?"

I stopped and craned my neck to see her halfway inside my house. "Yeah?"

Tala's face twisted in concern, her deep-set eyes tired but bright with curiosity. "I don't know if this helps, but I heard a man's voice with the woman before she screamed."

"Yeah." I sighed. "Kai walked her out. But he didn't see what happened."

Her long, silver hair blew back from her face with the force of another icy gust. "It didn't sound like Kai."

Alistair. He must have ran back to his car after attacking her.

"This man sounded older," she said, touching her fingertips to her throat. "You know, with a harsh voice that only comes from years of use."

Not Alistair. I resisted the urge to groan in front of Tala. She only wanted to help, but the piece she added to the puzzle didn't fit. In fact, it didn't even match the colors of the puzzle's picture.

But it did clear Scarlet from the wild accusation I'd thrown at her only hours ago. I owed her an apology. Whatever she was hiding likely didn't relate to Christa's murder. I knew I needed to admit that, as much as I wanted to blame anyone other than Kai.

"I'll look into it, thank you." With that, I cupped my stomach and carefully made my way down the stone steps. Either Jack braced me against the night's chill or the crazy weather had finally lifted, if only a few degrees.

By the time I scanned the sight of Christa's murder and walked over to where our car was parked, sweat had gathered on my brow. I bunched the hoodie's sleeve up to my elbows and then cupped beneath my belly.

A crawling sensation trickled up the back of my neck. I stepped out from between the cars and checked the parking lot again. Nobody was around. Even the shades and curtains on the nearby condos were pulled shut. Still, I felt eyes on me.

"Hello?" I asked and waited for a response.

Nothing.

I circled the edge of the small parking lot, checking the children's play structure and the alley. When my search didn't find a soul, I returned to the spot where I'd hidden the murder weapon.

"Okay, I have to crouch now so it's time to become Mister Winter," I said, speaking to my stomach. Jack didn't listen—probably the first act of a lifetime of ignoring his mom's hint drops. "Be lighter?" I begged. When that didn't work, I tried blowing on my skin. My breath wasn't cold enough. Either my son or his magic didn't want to obey.

"Fine, but if I can't get back up after this, I'm blaming you."

Jack responded with a swift kick to my ribcage. I rolled my eyes and popped a squat. The pressure of my stomach against my sternum forced a huff from my throat.

I peered under the car but found nothing other than concrete and oil stains.

"Where in the wonderland did it go?" I squeaked.

Relief flooded me as I spied the iron object halfway hidden by the back tire. I pulled the sleeve of my sweatshirt over my fingers and used it as a napkin to protect from fingerprints. I grunted and reached for it, feeling the cold metal in my grasp even through the fabric.

When I pulled it out, the dim light of the streetlamps illuminated the dried blood at the crook. I turned it over, examining the dark, crusted liquid.

The sweatshirt left a piece of green lint stuck to it.

"Really great, Mari," I chided myself. "Way to make Kai look even more guilty."

I grimaced as I used the sleeve to wipe everything off, even the blood. It'd at least smear Kai's fingerprints to make them unrecogniz-able in case the detective returned to retrieve the weapon. Carefully, I set the tire iron on the ground where it'd been witnessed by both the detective and Scarlet.

A sigh escaped me. This search yielded nothing helpful other than the realization that I needed Scarlet's help. She'd come into her own as an investigator while my skills had taken a break.

"Not to mention the fairy tale aspect," I said to my stomach. I couldn't ignore the fact that Christa was not only a character, but she knew who she'd become and about the magic under her control. If, in fact, her death related to her role as the Snow Queen, Scarlet would have the most experience nailing down the storybook side of the case. I'd had the hood most recently, but she had centuries of experience under her metaphorical belt and had even insisted she felt the story aura magic in past cases.

With the weapon clean, I replaced the tire iron to the concrete about where the detective had first seen it. I dug into my back pocket and produced my phone. Or so I thought. I'd been carrying both mine and Kai's cells and had accidentally grabbed his.

I pulled out mine and shot Scarlet a text.

I'm sorry for what I said. It feels like you're hiding something and I'm already on edge. But those aren't excuses for me to throw around murder accusations. I need your help on this case. P.S. I forgot to tell you, the rift ripped.

When it showed the message delivered, I stacked Kai's phone on top of mine and started investigating. I kept my eyes on the screen as I made my way back to the stairs. His text still struck me as unusual, even with his recent fairy tale changes. It didn't matter how distant we'd felt lately, he still cracked jokes in serious situations or reminded me he loved me through any anger between us.

I'll find you... it said. Find me where? I was a walking whale living in the same condo we'd shared for a decade. There was no amount of searching involved. It wasn't the language he'd use. Did this mysterious witness woman tell him to write it?

I swiped through the apps on his phone, trying to find any clues. Kai had left the phone by our park bench. Did he leave any other breadcrumbs in peculiar places that only I'd understand?

With my eyes on the screen, I took the stone steps slowly, catching my breath at each landing. The search through his texts gave me no new information. I tapped on a mobile food order app we loved to use for date nights at home.

At the top, he'd 'favorited' a restaurant we'd only eaten at once. We'd both hated it because the portions were way too small for our foodie love. It was a bougie place, too fancy for our palates.

"That's odd." But I made a mental note of it, anyway.

Kai liked Eternity Eatery. I didn't even like the nonsensical name that tried to stand out among the hundreds of other bougie restaurants in San Francisco, much less their food.

By the time I reached the top of the staircase, my pocket buzzed. Scarlet's face covered the screen, and I swiped to answer.

"Apology accepted," she said before I could greet her.

"I really am sorry." I bit my tongue. It wasn't the time to bring up the secret she'd been hiding. "Will you meet me at the rift? I think Storyland's magic has changed. I think—" I sighed. "It's affecting people differently after the hood mixed with it."

The other line fell silent, joining quiet snowflakes that dusted from the sky. Kai had seen snowflakes when there were none.

"Scar?"

"Okay," she finally said with exasperated force. "I'll meet you at the park."

The call cut and my screen blinked. I tucked both phones into my pockets and stared at the three flights of steps I'd just climbed.

"If only she'd called before I scaled the mountain." I took a deep breath and started the long waddle down the stairs. Then up the street. I shot Tala a quick message that I'd be back in about an hour and shoved my hands into the coat's pockets.

Though I couldn't feel the cold, unless it crystallized around my stomach from within, I didn't want to risk frostbite. It seemed with every step I took; the snowfall grew thicker.

My heart fluttered for no reason. Maybe I'd just gotten too out of shape and couldn't handle the hurried walk. A prickly feeling crawled up my neck. I scanned the street, spying only a young woman who sang along to the music in her car at a stoplight. No other pedestrians braved the weather.

I was alone.

"Except for you," I said, patting my stomach.

And someone else? The feeling of being watched followed me. I pushed on and stepped onto the path that led into the park. The sooner I met up with Scarlet, the sooner I'd feel the safety of numbers in case my senses were right.

A thin layer of snow blanketed the playground and benches. I spotted the small diamond shape of the rift and made my way to the center of Pioneer Park. Though it was already a quiet night because of the cold, the snow seemed to block all sound as sporadic noises from car engines faded.

I stopped in front of the rift and waited for Scarlet. The hood hadn't frayed any further. It remained tugged open where Wendy had peered through. My phone lit up with a confirmation from Tala that she'd received my text.

Thumbs up emoji See you in an hour.

In the snowy calm of the park, footsteps broke the silence.

I turned to greet Scarlet, but a movement rushed up against the side of my face and stopped me. The thwack of a hit sent searing pain through my ear. The weight in my stomach instantly lifted when Jack turned to cold.

Time slowed as everything went black and my legs crumpled beneath me.

Chapter Nine

"Let me be that I am and seek not to alter me."

— William Shakespeare

The sound of a man's voice confirmed my suspicions. Not only had he followed me, the stalker could be the same man Tala had heard with Christa. Which meant…*am I dead?*

I peeled my eyes open to the sight of branches hanging high above me. They reached their tips together, blocking the sky. A thin layer of snow clung to the leaves and my stomach iced over as a light breeze swept through the park. Relief flooded me after Jack's confirmation that he was okay. But what about me?

Of course you're not dead, Dumbo. How else would I have heard the voice of my attacker? With sudden awareness, I shot forward.

A rush of sharp pain bolted through my temples, and spots dotted my vision. My fingers instinctively touched at the source, coming back wet with blood.

"Relax," the man said.

My heart skipped a beat as my mind tried to catch up with the situation. I blinked the spots away and focused on the face in front of me.

Thick brows furrowed over gray eyes as he scanned me. Almost translucent skin revealed blue veins in his temples where hair hadn't grown in decades. My brain finally caught up with the sight of the medical examiner's familiar face.

"Reese?" I tried to make sense of where he'd come from. Why was he here? I spied the diamond shape of the rift to my right, hovering over my head.

"You were hit," Scarlet's voice cut through my thoughts.

I dabbed at the blood crusting on my ear. "How long was I out?" I glanced from Scarlet to Reese whose neck hump looked more pronounced as he hunched over me.

He gently pulled my hand away from the wound and examined my head. "Only a few moments," he said. "The good news is that the impact doesn't seem severe. You're bleeding because your earring was dislodged and pulled the lobe. You fell to the side which may have helped protect your baby but you'll need to get checked by an OBGYN as soon as possible."

OBGYNs who don't believe me. Thankfully, I felt a firm kick as Jack shifted from his frosty state to feisty baby again. Who had dared to hit a pregnant woman? Definitely a killer.

"Did you see who attacked me?" I asked, twisting to scan the park. Reese grabbed my head and yanked me back.

"Sorry," he mumbled once he realized how rough he'd been. "I'm don't deal with live bodies often."

Scarlet wiped at her brow and straightened from her place on her knees. "No, I don't know who it was. But I wish I did. I feel awful, I got here before you and called Reese to come look at the rift too. Since he's still, well—"

"The Hunchback of Notre Dame," Reese said. He'd always acknowledged his role as Quasimodo with a matter-of-fact approach. Though his storybook character's tale ended in tragedy, he'd requested that I not interfere because it was better to love and know Esmeralda than not at all.

"I met Reese at the entrance on the other side of the park," she explained. "When we walked back together, we found you on the ground and I only saw someone running away."

The sharp pain from when I'd sat up dulled to a throbbing ache. I dabbed at my earlobe where blood started crusting. My earring slipped easily from the stretched piercing hole. The emerald stud had turned dark with blood and the post was bent from the impact of my attacker's hit. The matching earrings Kai had bought for Wendy and I needed to be replaced now.

"Did you see what they looked like?" I asked as I tucked the broken jewelry into my pocket.

"Only from a distance," Scarlet said. "I'm guessing a man since they were stocky, and definitely taller than you and me. Is your wallet missing?"

I patted my other pocket to find nothing had been taken and shook my head. The throbbing intensified with the movement.

"I was being followed," I said.

"Followed?" Scarlet cocked her head. A waterfall of red curls tumbled over her shoulder. "By the attacker? Or is Kai trying to find you?"

After a steadying breath, I met her gaze. "From the crime scene."

"Do you think it's the same person who killed Christa?" she asked.

I pinched the bridge of my nose and tried to will the headache away. "I don't know."

"Wait!" Scarlet shot to her feet. Reese stopped his examination of my injury only long enough to see where Scarlet had disappeared to.

Snow crunched beneath her feet as she took off in the direction she'd said my attacker went. Scarlet dropped to one knee and pulled her curls from her face with one hand.

"They match!" she shouted. Eagerly, she pointed to the snow. "This is the same pattern from the shoe print at the crime scene."

"Now I'm definitely not letting you walk back home," Reese said as he stood. He wiped his hands and returned thin-rimmed glasses to his nose.

I squinted up at him through the pounding pain. The rift caught my eye, or rather, the hood. Thought of throbbing injuries faded as I focused on the fabric.

The red velvet corner had been stretched out of shape. The thread at the edge of the fabric hung further from the rift's pulsing flesh. Unlike when Wendy had yanked on it, the hood only looked stretched rather than unraveled or removed from where it was sewn into the rift. Someone had tampered with it since we were here.

"It changed." I pointed to the rift. When I curled my feet underneath me, it took both Scarlet and Reese's help to haul me upright. Jack didn't help by turning into his frosty form, of course. Such was the life of a mother.

Carefully, I pinched the fabric and peeled it back to look inside Storyland. I didn't see the world of wonder that Wendy had. Instead, I only saw rippling colors and a pulsing fleshy rift. The seam tying the hood to the rift unraveled and peeled away at my touch. I yanked my hand back. Whoever had tugged on it either loosened the seal, or the hood still only obeyed my touch. The stretched nature of the fabric indicated they'd tried to pull on it but it hadn't given away.

"Changed how?" Scarlet asked. The slight quiver in her voice caught me off guard.

I peeled my eyes from the rift to glance at her. Wrinkles creased at her brow and she raked her fingers through the ends of her hair, pulling hard enough to straighten a lock of curls. The last time I'd seen her this nervous was her first day as an intern at Bay Side Media.

"Are you okay?" I asked. With the million other worries on my mind, I'd failed to see my best friend's obvious worry. Worry that was likely masked by blame and anger during our earlier fight. "What is it?"

Her throat rippled, and she folded her arms. The protective stance made her look like a child who'd broken a rule and didn't want to own up to it. She drew a sharp breath and looked at the rift.

Reese peered at us over his glasses, shifting his gaze from her to me without a word.

"You really won't tell me?" I prodded. Sure, I needed patience with whatever battled within her. But we didn't have time on our side and the ache in my head, though dulled, was a constant reminder that I was in danger.

"Why don't we go to the morgue?" Reese said. He didn't wait for us stubborn women to follow. The up and down movement of his unsteady gait bobbed in my peripheral. I kept my eyes on Scarlet who stared at the rift.

"You'd better be following me, Mari," Reese called over his shoulder. "I need to examine you and you're clearly not safe here." He continued limping toward the exit opposite from where I'd entered Pioneer Park. A small pathway led further down Main where it was only a short walk to the new building he worked at. "And Scarlet, you and I both know you need help. So, let's get on with it."

Need help? My lips parted. Scarlet dropped her arms and followed in Reese's wake with me at her side.

Reese stopped and turned. With one flick of his arm, Scarlet knew to flank me. Together they kept me safe, each at my side. Wind blew at our backs as we shuffled from the park.

Patches of snow still hid in scattered areas off the concrete trail where bark and bushes covered the ground. Most of it had melted and soaked into the earth but the remains reminded me of Christa's power —a power more intense and influential on our world than any I'd witnessed from storybook characters before.

Was this the change the Brothers Grimm had warned me of? I knew the hood was only a temporary hold on Storyland's magic, but I'd hoped I had more time. I needed to give birth to this baby and deal with the story tangling my husband's mind before I threw myself into others' lives again. One day, soon, I'd be forced into sealing fairy tale endings again. For today, the pain throbbing through my skull took precedence.

I'd let Reese examine me, then we'd return to the rift and backtrack whoever had stalked me.

Reese opened the door to his home base where the city stored dead bodies. Cool air rushed into our faces from the air conditioner that permanently ran. A single metal table sat in the center of the room. The wall to our right looked identical to a doctor's office with a long counter, plenty of drawers, and a sink. Stacks of wide drawers lined the back wall—temporary coffins kept cold for lifeless bodies.

The chill of the morgue didn't bother me. It wasn't enough to trigger Jack's frost either. I followed Reese and leaned against his rolling chair. He clicked a light and shined the beam into my eye. Once he was satisfied that my pupils didn't reveal a concussion, he questioned my symptoms. Was I dizzy or sleepy?

"Are you feeling confused?" he asked.

My gaze shifted to the redhead hovering in the morgue's corner. The former Keeper of Stories had changed so much, from confident villain killer to a regular young woman with centuries of a complex past.

"I'm confused about everything," I said. I blinked and met Reese's gray eyes. "But, no, I'm fine." Since the throbbing dulled and the piercing hole only slightly stung now, it didn't count as a lie.

"Good." He set the light on the shiny metal table behind me, stood, and sauntered to the morgue's freezer. The wall of drawers stood taller than him, making his hunched body look even shorter. "Now, let's get to the meat of this investigation. Christa was definitely no normal human. My examination revealed that the blow she took was powerful enough to have shattered her entire head, but bruising patterns show she hit the ground while she was still alive. She wasn't immortal, but she was unnaturally strong and I suspect whoever killed her had to match that strength. I'm guessing fast too. Based on how her heart looked, it pumped blood twice as fast as a regular human heart, which unfortunately meant she died quickly from the blood loss." With a sigh and an apologetic look, he met my gaze. "You might not like to hear this Mari, considering what we know about your husband, but Christa's killer must have been a storybook character. The man who ran away from the attack matches the murderer. From the angle of Christa's wounds, I've determined the killer is tall, almost certainly a man. So are we confident enough to say your attacker is the man who murdered her?" He knocked his knuckles against the drawer.

All of his information only confirmed what I'd already suspected.

Though I'd still never suspect Kai. He was a character, but not *the* character who ended our OBGYN's life.

I rubbed the heels of my palms against my eyes and sighed. "I don't know for sure if it's the same person. It's just a feeling since I thought they—he—" I corrected as I glanced at Scarlet. She'd called the attacker a man based on his body's size and shape. "He followed me from the scene of the crime."

"Feelings are powerful," Scar piped up. She stepped out of the shadowy corner of the morgue and paced in front of the door with a lock of curls twisted around her finger so tightly the skin went white. "Especially for the Keeper."

Though her pacing and gestures expressed anxiety, her voice came out low and intense. It brought me back many years, when she wore the hood and I saw her as a threat—a morally gray magical being. But time and assimilation into modern society had eroded her intensity, and lack of the hood had stripped all of her powers.

"Okay, you're being weird," I said. A huff escaped me as I forced myself to stand and face Scarlet. Jack felt heavier than ever with his head resting on my bladder.

"I know." She squeezed her eyes shut.

"Time to get some help, Miss Scarlet," Reese said. He'd always addressed her with a slight formal air and I couldn't blame him. When he'd met her, she was a powerful Keeper of Stories who'd created a portal into his office. "The story aura never completely left this world. I'm proof of that."

"Yes, but new characters—" she cut herself off with her jaw snapped shut and a shake of her head.

"You don't believe it's possible for people to become characters anymore," I guessed. "If it's because of the hood, I can tell you, the Brothers Grimm predicted this. It was never meant to solve the story aura. I just need more time..." my voice faded as I looked down and rubbed my palm over my stomach.

Two years of carrying this child left me feeling weak and vulnerable. Couldn't the story magic just wait a little longer before it returned to ruin more lives? A chill—not one from the cold—trickled down my spine and goosebumps prickled along the back of my arms.

"Miss Scarlet…" Reese prodded. "Tell the Keeper what you told me."

"It's impossible," she mumbled. She twisted and untwisted her hair around her finger, pulling tighter each time. If she kept going, she'd cut off all blood from the tip of her finger.

My hand instinctively flexed as the muscles remembered an old habit. When I wore the hood, I'd always twirl the string the same way Scarlet played with her hair. That comfort was gone now.

"Storyland magic has definitely changed," I said. "I don't know how the hood affected it but we know it has because the Snow Queen died before her story ended. Plus, her magic was not like any I've seen considering she turned this entire city into her snowy domain. Even the rift looks different."

"I just can't believe it," she said with a shake of her head.

"Why?"

"Because if that's true, then that means something horrible." Finally, she looked at me, unblinking.

Was she worried for Kai? Did this mean she still believed he'd brutally attacked our storybook OBGYN? First, I needed her to know the magic still existed, and then that the magic had changed.

I waddled to Scarlet and blocked her path of pacing. When she stopped in front of me, I reached for her hand. Gently, I unwound the lock of hair tangled around her finger and laid her hand on my stomach.

Please, Jack.

Thankfully, her hand was ice cold and my son reacted. His magic created a layer of frost on my belly, dampening the shirt underneath my hoodie.

"Okay, okay, I get it," she said.

"So? Can you admit Kai is a character?"

Scarlet folded her arms and shoved past me to continue pacing. "If I admit Kai is a character or your baby, or whatever, then that means I have to admit *I'm* a character."

"What?"

She stopped and pointed to her own stomach. "I'm starving!"

"Okay?" I didn't know how skipping lunch related to storybook magic. I glanced at Reese who waved for Scarlet to continue but she pursed her lips. Since she didn't talk, I filled the silence. "So, get a burger? We'll stop at McDonald's for a quick meal and then we'll get on with the investigation before I get attacked again." I shuffled toward the door, trying to hold in my pee since every step seemed to push Jack's skull further into my bladder.

"I'm not a hungry child you can throw a Happy Meal at," she scoffed. I bit my lip before a rude comment slipped out. *You could have fooled me.* Judging by her stomping feet and scowling face, I'd call it a tantrum.

"Then what do you want to eat?"

Before I moved another step, Scarlet marched up to me and grabbed my shoulders. Her eyes looked wild with fear and frustration. "Don't you get it?"

"I really don't—"

"I'm the witch from Hansel and Gretel!" Her fingernails dug into my shoulder and her arms shook slightly. "I'm hungry and nothing I eat satisfies me. I know I'm a character because this hunger is consuming my mind. All I can think about is this craving to eat and nothing makes it stop. "

My eyes that bugged now. Carefully, I peeled her hands off of me and then I shot Reese a look.

"So, you want to eat children?" I asked.

"Ew, no!" She squealed and her hand shot to her mouth.

"Isn't that what the witch does?" My gaze shifted between them. Reese confirmed my fear with a curt nod.

Scarlet nearly crumpled. Her shoulders dropped and arms fell limp at her sides. With her head rolled back and eyes fixed on the ceiling, she let out a groan. "I hate this. I hate myself."

"But the stories find people who match the characters—"

"Do they?" She interrupted. "You said so yourself, the magic has changed."

"Yes, but—"

"Kill me." Another interruption. Once I got her talking, it seemed she wouldn't stop. She grabbed my shoulders again before I could dodge her hands. Thankfully, it didn't last, and she released her death grip on me.

Without another word, she marched to the counter behind the metal table. The drawers beneath the countertop banged as she searched for something. Once she found it, she slammed the drawer shut and spun around wielding a scalpel in her grasp. Her knuckles turned white with how tightly she gripped the sharp object. It caught the overhead light and shined in my eyes.

"I'm mortal, right? So kill me," she begged. "Kill me before I become a monster."

I crossed my arms. "Yes, because murdering you in front of the medical examiner is a brilliant plan," I said. I kept my voice monotonous, calm and flat. "That will solve everything."

"Fine." Scarlet spun around, sending her long curls over her shoulder. She swung the morgue's door open and marched through. After exchanging glances, we hurried to follow.

"What're you doing?" I waddled along beside her, doing my best to catch up without peeing my pants.

"Going to the rift," she said without looking at me. "I know you're too stubborn to do this one simple thing. But a reminder of what's worse might kick your butt into gear."

Simple? Killing someone was anything but simple.

I HUFFED and puffed as we entered Pioneer Park again. Trying to keep pace with Scarlet had me choking on my spit.

I coughed and swallowed. "Care to explain your plan?" The question came out in fits between gasps of breath.

"Because," she said, "if you won't kill me, then you need the hood." Scarlet marched across the concrete to the center of the park and curled her fingers around the piece of fabric that flapped in the breeze. When she pulled, it didn't give.

"Ugh, I knew it," she scoffed and waved her hand at me. "You have to take it."

"I won't," I said. Now that we stopped, I sucked in enough air to breathe normally. If the hood didn't block the rift, more stories would flood through and take over our world. I didn't have the time or energy to track them right now.

"You won't kill the witch who tries to eat two innocent kids either," she spoke through her teeth. "But once you're the Keeper, I trust you will. You'll see the aura and it will show you the truth. The truth will lead you to Hansel and Gretel. In the real fairy tale, they outwit the villain, but the magic is changed now. If the Snow Queen can die—the queen of eternity—then who knows what I'll be able to do as the witch?"

"I doubt you're the witch—wait, did you say eternity?" The word triggered a thought. I dug into my back pocket and produced my phone. Since it was the wrong one, I gripped it between my middle and pointer finger and pulled out Kai's phone. I tapped his password into the screen and clicked on the mobile food app.

Eternity Eatery.

I knew Kai didn't like that restaurant. If this were anyone else, I'd think myself crazy for considering it a clue. But I knew my husband. We'd solved many mysteries together and had dined at dozens of restaurants in town. This wasn't a mistake or a coincidence. He'd favorited only one restaurant, and the one we disliked the most—the one with the same word Scarlet used to describe the woman Kai was accused of murdering.

"Why did you call her that?" I asked, almost breathless again. "Why eternity?"

"I told you to do better research," she snapped. I didn't take her anger personally, knowing now that it was born of desperation and fear. "In Hans Christian Andersen's original tale, the Snow Queen demands that the boy Kai use pieces of ice to spell a word." She met my gaze with nearly the same intensity she'd had as the Keeper.

Scarlet was definitely a character. How had I not seen it? The change in her was clear now. She'd become demanding and angry with the lack of control over her life—just as Kai had reacted whenever I'd suggested he was the boy in *The Snow Queen*.

I never stopped to consider the emotional turmoil it must cause to know one's fate had become entangled with fiction. Was that the cause of Scarlet's dissonance with Carlos too? And where was he the moment the Christa died? As another suspect on the list, I couldn't ignore his presence at the crime scene.

"That word is eternity," she said. As soon as she said it, it seemed the clouds in my mind parted and the sun shone a light on a clue. The odd restaurant choice in his mobile food app matched his fairy tale.

"Kai left me a message," I said, holding out the phone. I tapped on the screen as if that explained everything. "He's admitting that he's Kai. This is him asking for help which means he knows he didn't kill Christa. Someone else must have written that confession." Words spilled out of my mouth now as I pieced the puzzle together. Knowing my husband so well helped me see the cracks in whoever had forced him to write the confession.It wasn't certain evidence, but it made the most sense in a chaotic case. I needed all the sane theories I could get right now. "I have to solve this. He needs me to solve this because he knows he didn't do it."

"Mari, did you hear *my* confession?" Scarlet asked. She jabbed her finger into her chest where the V-neck shirt revealed the milky white skin below her collarbone.

"If Kai is Kai, then it probably means the stories still find those who match the original characters. He was innocent, playful, and full of love until the shards of the troll mirror's glass changed him. Christa was cold and controlling and she became the Snow Queen."

"It's true," Reese said, finally catching up with us. He winced with every limp and I hated that we dragged him out of his comfort zone again. The poor man deserved a bit of peace before he succumbed to Quasimodo's tragic and mysterious fate. "I'm still the same character. The magic might have changed, but I didn't because my characteristics match that of the Hunchback of Notre Dame."

"See?" I pointed at Reese to emphasize my point. "You're a character, Scar, but I'm willing to bet you're no witch. Help me solve Christa's murder. Free Kai from this accusation and I'll free you from whatever story has taken hold of your life. *The Snow Queen* is one of the only stories we're sure of right now. We can use it to understand the new magic before we jump to crazy conclusions about you."

She released a shaky breath. "And if I am the witch, will you kill me?"

"One step at a time. Pinning the murderer is our only focus right now. He's a character, too. Let's find out if his personality predetermined him to become a villain."

After several moments of silence, Scarlet finally sighed. It felt like I was on the edge of my seat waiting for confirmation that she'd help. I wished I was on the edge of a toilet seat. It took everything I had not to prod her to answer faster so I could run off to find a restroom.

I crossed my legs and did a little wiggle to keep from wetting myself like a toddler. Thankfully, a slight breeze triggered Jack into his frosty state and the pressure of his skull released from my bladder.

She let out a small groan that led into her response. "I'm in."

With Scarlet on my side, and the clue in Kai's phone, I was more hopeful than ever.

Chapter Ten

"Nothing clears up a case so much as stating it to another person."

— Arthur Conan Doyle

For the next half a day, Scarlet, Reese, and I became The Three Musketeers. Of course, we were not swordsmen, or characters in the novel by Alexandre Dumas, but we worked as a team to protect San Francisco the way the musketeers protected France.

Or rather, protection by association. If we found and stopped Christa's killer, we'd make the city safer.

While we waited for more information from the detective, and a return call from Christa's boyfriend, we took to fairy tales. Original stories by the Brothers Grimm, Hans Christian Andersen, and more buried my coffee table. I pulled off my reading glasses, a newer addition after years of squinting at my scribbled sticky notes. The ache in my head flared again after scanning too many books and Jack flip-flopped in my stomach.

I took a break from paperbacks and pulled out Kai's phone. For the fifth time, I scoured his apps for more clues. Nothing stood out to me about his whereabouts, though I made a note of the only other odd thing I'd found.

Kai's most recent Google tag: Blair Danes. Who was Blair Danes? Apparently, my husband didn't know either, and that was why he'd taken to the largest online search engine in the world. For now, I assumed Blair was the woman who'd offered to help him—the *witness*.

The online search yielded nothing, but a few abandoned social media pages, an obituary, and a leader from a country on the other side of the world. Nothing matched the likelihood of a lady in a San Francisco condominium complex. Since we'd determined the murderer a man, Blair was off the hook.

"We've gone through everything," Reese said as he swiped his palm over his thinning hair. A tattered copy of *The Little Mermaid* tumbled off a stack of hardbacks after he'd tossed it too far and missed the pile. He leaned back in the chair and sighed. "There is no alternative storyline to *The Snow Queen* where she dies and no villain who'd want to kill her."

Except for a boy out for revenge. I shoved the thought away because I'd never believe Kai capable of taking another life, story aura or not. Besides, the original tale ended happily with Gerda saving the boy Kai just before he was about to freeze to death.

"What about from another tale?" I asked. My finger trailed the stacks of books. None of the titles jumped out at me as clearly as the last two names on my list. If only Detective Wilhelm would return our calls, we'd be able to pay a visit to the man I suspected the most. Even knowing his name, Alistair wasn't easy to find.

I brushed hair from my face, lifted my head, and landed my gaze across the room. In the kitchen, Scarlet brought a nearly empty pot of coffee to her face. She frowned at it and shook the remaining liquid then popped the top. After trying a sip straight from the pot, her frown deepened. Finally, she spun around to grab one of Wendy's juice boxes from the fridge.

With questioning Alistair on hold, the name of the only other suspect burned a hole through my thoughts. The only problem was, Carlos had no motive.

"Hey, Scar," I said. "I have to ask this. Do you know where Carlos was when Christa died?"

Scarlet swung her hips around the edge of the counter and furrowed her brows at me. She marched across the room and flopped onto the couch beside me. All the while, she held my gaze and stabbed the pointy end of the plastic straw into the juice box.

"He was on his way here," she said. "Don't pull a *Detective Wilhelm* on me and start throwing accusations at anybody around."

I raised my palms in surrender, and she visibly relaxed. "I get it, he doesn't have motive. But he was at the scene before Alistair."

After a nice long sip of apple juice, Scarlet smacked her lips. "Because Murder Boyfriend probably ditched the scene and then came back as an innocent, whereas Carlos is actually innocent. Early, but innocent."

I pulled my leg onto the couch and turned sideways to face her "Early?"

When she polished off the apple juice, the box crumpled. "If you want to know why he tried to beat me here, you'll need to ask him yourself. I have my suspicions. It's already stressed him out enough to know that I might know what he doesn't want me to know. He was upset when I confronted him about it. I'm just emotional... you know? Anyway, he has a secret, but it has nothing to do with murder."

I didn't doubt that. Quickly, I shot him a text to ask exactly what Scarlet had suggested. My phone pinged with a prompt response.

Carlos: I needed advice without Scar overhearing.

Three little typing lines popped up, then disappeared, and then popped up again. I waited, cocking my head at the phone for whatever he hesitated to share.

Carlos: I want to propose.

Spit lodged in my throat as I gasped. The phone slipped from my hand and fell between couch cushions while the choking launched me into a bout of coughing.

"Whoa there!" Scarlet sat up and patted my back. "Are you okay?"

I continued coughing and gave her a thumbs up. My head throbbed where the attacker had whacked me. When the coughing subsided, I took a deep breath.

"I'm good," I assured them… Good as a girl could be after two years of pregnancy and her husband missing.

I wished I could celebrate the happy news—the romance that'd blossomed between Scarlet and Carlos. Now wasn't the time to stop and smell the bouquet of bridal roses. Like many other parts of life, this needed to be put on hold.

"Let's focus on the case." A huff escaped me. My giant belly pressed into my sternum as I leaned forward and slid *The Snow Queen* off the stack of books.

I flipped through the pages for the hundredth time. It seemed I knew every illustration of the boy Kai and the queen herself. I skimmed the beginning of each section starting with the devil who created an evil mirror and ending with a passage from the Bible. None of it helped. *The boy Kai gets angry. The devil is called a troll. The queen of winter has no real goal or purpose in the plot. The girl Gerda saves her brother's life.* The whole thing drove me nuts. What piece of the story were we missing? And why didn't the real Gerda respond to my texts?

"I've got something," Scarlet said. A grin spread across her face, stretching her ruby lips to her rosy cheeks. She flipped the laptop around for us to see and we both leaned in for a closer look. The screen displayed dozens of images of shoe prints. Scarlet's pointed fingernail tapped at one in particular. "This is the print from the snow and the crime scene. Since it's a simple pattern with a high arch its likely from a boot rather than the complex soles of a sneaker."

"Excellent work, Miss Scarlet," Reese said.

I could only stare at her in awe. Even at the height of my career as an investigative journalist, I'd never identified shoe prints. Centuries of tracking story characters, had helped her home in on the details of crime scenes.

The discovery was impressive but not enough to solve anything yet.

The screen of Reese's phone lit up on the coffee table between towers of books. It buzzed until he reached for it. He stood and took the call, shuffling back and forth behind the chair.

I slapped the book shut and pinched the bridge of my nose. With careful focus, I imagined the pieces of the puzzle in specific colors.

Alistair is red, the clearest suspect. But which character could he possibly be? And why kill his girlfriend?

In orange, I mentally noted the fact that someone had followed me from the crime scene and then attacked me.

I sucked in a breath. "Okay, so we know the killer is a storybook character based on their strength. We know it's a man and that he stalked me to the park, so he still hangs around the crime scene. And we know—"

"What might have killed Christa," Reese interrupted, finishing my sentence. He shoved his phone into his pocket and offered us a curt nod. "That was the detective. He has a theory about the murder weapon and wants me to compare his ideas to Christa's wounds."

I scooted to the edge of the cushion. "What type of weapon?" The tire iron flashed in my mind's eye. Good thing I'd already wiped Kai's fingerprints.

Reese shrugged. "He's done this before. If he's desperate, the ideas could be anything from an ice skate to a—" he waved his hand in the general direction of the coffee table. "A hardback book."

"Did you tell him to call me back?"

Reese swung the door open and limped through, pausing just past the threshold. "I did. But no promises. He said he doesn't trust you considering the circumstances."

I should have known the detective still wanted to throw accusations at me. At least that deflected him from looking into the man who held the actual murder weapon. All I needed was a little more time to clear Kai's name.

"Mari," Reese said, cutting through my thoughts. "Detective Wilhelm said he thinks you're involved."

My stomach twisted. That sounded like more than lazy accusations. Did the detective find evidence that incriminated Kai?

Reese frowned. "And he warned me not to talk to you." With that, he pulled the door shut behind him.

Scarlet sighed and stood. "You know what that means?"

It means time is running out.

I nodded. "Yeah, we need to get to the station and tell another officer that Detective Wilhelm forgot to give us the address."

"Yep."

Maybe it wasn't right to tell a white lie for information, but desperate times…

"We need to talk to Alistair like yesterday," I said.

"Yep," she repeated.

I followed Scarlet's actions, locating a jacket, my shoes, and keys, and prepared to leave. We hurried from the condo and down to the street.

The brisk walk kept me warm—hot, actually. While Scarlet kept her coat on, I stripped mine, unbothered by the chilly breeze that turned her nose and ears red. Even the sidewalk couldn't handle the weather. The concrete had turned slick with a layer of ice. Carefully, and as quickly as possible, we maneuvered across the frozen ground, using patches of remaining snow to step on when we could.

At the station, our mission proved easier than expected. With a bit of smooth-talking, we worked Alistair's address out of another officer and then headed to his house. On the way, we stopped at Wendy's school just in time for pickup.

She tagged along, asking about her daddy, Auntie Scar's new life— whatever that meant—and if we could get a Happy Meal. In order to avoid answering the first question, we took a quick detour to McDonalds. The cheeseburger, fries, and plastic toy kept her distracted long enough to accept the answer that daddy was simply busy on a trip.

When we arrived at Alistair's upscale apartment, Scarlet knocked on the door. A swift breeze rushed through the outdoor hallway while we waited for a response. Wendy munched the last of her french fries and rocked back and forth on her sneakers.

"Why're we here?" she asked. "I forgot."

"Just to ask a friend some questions," I said.

The 'friend' finally swung the door open. Alistair towered over us as he stood at the threshold wearing no shirt and a pair of gym shorts. With a white towel, he wiped sweat from his face and chest. His massive frame filled the doorway, but I glimpsed the spacious apartment through his armpit as he wiped his forehead.

Inside, walls of bookshelves went from the floor to the ceiling, surrounding a banquet table at the center of the library-like room. A place this large on this side of town would cost a fortune. The bit of information we'd gleaned from the officer down at the station included the fact that Alistair had no job, which meant he was likely born into money. If he'd killed Christa, financial gain certainly wasn't the motive.

He wrinkled his brow and shifted his gaze between us. "Do I know you?"

"We're investigating the murder of Christa Lang. Can we ask you a few questions?" I asked.

Alistair crumpled the towel in his fist, nearly squeezing the sweat out of it. He jabbed his finger at my face and frowned. "I already told the other detective everything I know. Why am I being harassed again if I have an alibi for—"

"Mommy?" Wendy interrupted Alistair's rant. To my surprise, the giant man clamped his jaw shut and stared down at my daughter. They blinked at one another for a moment before she opened her mouth again. "Why does his hair look like fur?"

Heat instantly warmed my cheeks. I pulled Wendy into me and offered Alistair an apologetic smile.

"I'm sorry. Did you say you have an alibi?" I continued.

He leaned against the door frame. "Yes, I was at Kobold's Coffee when—"

"Mommy?" Wendy said again.

I patted her shoulder and forced another smile. "Not now—"

"Are princes and princesses real?" she asked, blinking up at me. I opened my mouth to respond but she didn't let me get a word in. "Because he looks like a prince. Or maybe a king."

Alistair stopped leaning and folded his muscular arms across his chest. A small smile flickered at the corner of his mouth but it quickly shifted to a grimace again. Wendy wasn't wrong. Alistair's impressive height, chiseled jaw, and ego all came together for a regal energy.

He backed into the apartment. "I don't have time for this. I've got a workout to finish."

"Wait!" My hand shot out to block him from closing the door. "Your alibi, would you mind sharing?"

His lip curled into what I could only describe as a snarl. "Coffee," he said, "I have the actual coffee cups with my name, Christa's name, and a timestamp for when I ordered."

"What about mobile pickup?" Scarlet asked. Leave it to the girl dating a former DoorDash driver to think of that loophole.

He groaned. "The baristas already told the other detective they all saw me in the shop. Besides, I thought the detective said he already had a clear suspect."

"Right," I lied. My brain worked overtime trying to plan a question that'd get him to spill more information. Did Detective Wilhelm have Kai pinned as a suspect? "We do." I glanced at Scarlet and hoped she'd follow my lead. "We just need to know if you can give us your description of the suspect."

"Look, I wasn't there. All I know is what that creeper cop told me. Christa was attacked by a patient's husband but they haven't found the guy."

Before I could process what he said, Alistair slammed the door in our faces. A rush of air swept hair from my face and my heart stalled, skipping beats.

It's official, Kai's the suspect. It seemed my heart had leaped into my throat. I couldn't breathe and my pulse thudded in my neck. Had Detective Wilhelm returned for the tire iron? Had I failed at clearing Kai's fingerprints?

With every beat of my heart, time slipped away. The detective had found evidence against my husband faster than I was gathering clues on the real murderer. With Alistair's alibi, I'd ran out of suspects.

"We need to go," I said, startling from my daze. If the detective didn't come back for the tire iron, I still had a chance to get rid of it and stall for more time—time I needed to uncover another suspect. The only other name I had left was the mysterious Blair Danes. Could she have worked with a man to frame Kai for Christa's murder? Maybe my husband's Google search held the key to finding a pair of killers.

Scarlet nodded and offered Wendy a piggyback ride. Wendy insisted she didn't want to hurt Auntie Scar and walked instead.

I mulled over the possibilities while we speed-walked back to the crime scene. Since the killer had the strength and speed of a storybook character, did that mean Blair Danes was a character too? Which fairy tales had two villains working together? And how did that crossover into *The Snow Queen*?

When we arrived home, I sent Wendy upstairs.

She stomped her feet and protested. "I want to help!"

Of course she did. Wendy took after me, already wanting to solve puzzles and help others. But she needed to enjoy soccer, spelling bees, and science experiments, not focus on murder mysteries and fairy tale villains. Someday, she'd likely follow in my footsteps. Today was not that day.

I brushed hair from her face and tucked it behind her ear. "I know," I said, "and I promise you can help with research when we go to the library."

At that, Wendy nodded, and Scarlet smiled. Scar knew exactly what that meant. Time wasn't on our side and without suspects to question, we'd return to hunting for a character who might have killed Christa. Or was the goal to frame Kai? Or maybe to get to me? All of those questions would be quicker and easier to answer if first we identified the character then tracked the plot of their story. Among books, we'd dig for obscure fairy tales and classic stories to find the answer to this case—after I hid the murder weapon.

Scarlet beckoned for Wendy to follow her to the condo while I spun the opposite direction. I cupped the bottom of my stomach and crouched when I reached the car. It took every bit of strength I had to get into the right position to look under our car.

Despite the uncomfortable position, I got a full view of the space beneath the SUV. Nothing but a discarded water bottle rolled along the concrete, pushed by the icy wind.

Once again, my heart found its way into my throat and I struggled to breathe.

The murder weapon was gone.

Chapter Eleven

"I wasted time, and now doth time waste me."

— William Shakespeare

Online birthing classes helped me deal with stress better than labor itself—if I ever went into labor. Each breath I took slowed my pulse and cleared my head. I paced the length of our living room while following the recommended inhale and exhale rhythm from the YouTube video on the TV.

Will the cops trace the tire iron back to Kai? They couldn't since it didn't belong to us. Right?

Wrong. If I hadn't wiped well enough, they could still pull my husband's fingerprints from the weapon…not to mention the fact that they found it under our car. What was I thinking when I'd hid it there?

It felt lazy to blame the mistake on my fuzzy pregnancy brain, but I couldn't deny the truth. As much as I wanted to stay one step ahead of the investigation, exhaustion from growing a magical human had me falling two steps behind.

I paced faster and lost time with the birthing class's instructions, breathing twice as fast now.

Wendy copied me, literally following in my footsteps. Where I stepped, she stepped. When I sucked in a breath, she popped a graham cracker shaped like a teddy bear into her mouth. Okay, so she didn't mirror my actions exactly—she was her own little person, after all.

"With all that walking I wouldn't be surprised if the baby falls out of you," Scarlet said. She curled her feet beneath her butt and sat on the couch crisscross applesauce style.

I stopped and glared at her. "Really helpful, Scar. Thanks."

The sudden halt made Wendy bump into my butt. Scarlet shrugged and pressed her phone to her ear.

"Honesty is the best policy," she said. "Let's not panic until we know for sure what evidence they have. I'm calling Esmeralda to see if she'll tell me about the weapon."

Officer Esmeralda had not only worked on investigations with me before, but she'd become a family friend. Unfortunately, after her divorce, we'd struggled to find time to get together. While she'd taken to dating, I was swamped with sleep.

I watched the woman in the birthing video and tried to resume the breathing techniques. When that didn't work, I continued pacing. Theories scrambled in my mind. *Next step, find Blair Danes and the man she's working with.*

I marched to the Coffee Table of Evidence and snatched Kai's phone from the edge. Quickly, I tapped his password into the screen and swiped through the apps again. I resumed pacing while scanning for any more clues. Nothing about Blair Danes came up on his social media apps or anywhere else. Still, I wanted to be thorough, even opening apps he never used like the files folder and TV streaming services.

With each swipe, my heart sank. No new clues guided me. Except for one. The last of several TV apps piqued my curiosity. Kai always had History Channel shows queued to watch. All Ancient Egyptian and Histories Mysteries shows were now removed from the queue. Only one show—one Kai would never watch—was saved for viewing.

Hannibal. I tapped the show's picture to double-check that it wasn't the ancient Hannibal from historic Rome. The description of the disturbing serial-killer character confirmed my creeping suspicion. Hannibal? As in *the* Hannibal that killed and ate people? My stomach curdled. What in the wonderland? I'd had enough mention of cannibalism with Scarlet's claim to be the witch from Hansel and Gretel's tale.

Kai would rather order grass at Eternity Eatery than watch this show. Did that make this single queue another clue?

A knock pounded against our front door and I jolted, nearly dropping the phone. A gasp escaped me as the sound echoed in the room. I shuffled to the door, kicking Wendy's shoes and backpack out of the way so I could pull it open.

A familiar, scowling face greeted me. With one hand at his belt, and the other gripping a pair of handcuffs, Detective Wilhelm looked ready to strike. My heart skipped a beat at the sight of his fingers curling around his gun.

"Step outside," he demanded.

"What?" I blinked at him.

The door across from our condo creaked open and Tala's face appeared in the crack.

"I heard banging," she said.

Detective Wilhelm ignored her. "Step outside. Now!"

"What's going on?" I asked. When my feet didn't budge, the detective reached out and gripped my wrist. His fingers felt like a vice ready to crush the bones in my hand.

Already off-balance from my basketball belly, I nearly fell into him as he yanked me across the threshold.

"It gives me no pleasure to arrest you again." He spit the words at my neck as he tugged on my arm and forced me to turn around.

"Wait, for what?" I asked. When I tried to twist and face him, he yanked harder on my arms.

"Are you resisting arrest?" His voice rang in my ears. Detective Wilhelm shoved me against the wall beside the front door.

Instinctively, I leaned forward to protect my stomach from squishing against the wall. Instead, my cheek and injured ear took the brunt of the pressure. I cringed at the pain of my barely healed earlobe pressed into the gray paint on the outside of the condo.

"Hey!" I found my voice though it sounded disembodied. It came out squeaky and weak—too startled for confidence.

Detective Wilhelm twisted my arms behind my back. The cold slap of the handcuffs hit my wrists.

Someone gasped. Or maybe it came from each of the three women who witnessed the detective's behavior. I twisted my neck, hoping to see Wendy had gone to the bathroom and or to play in her room.

She shouldn't see this.

But she did. Enormous eyes stared up at me as little feet found their way to the threshold between our home and the hallway. My heart dropped to my stomach at the sight of her worried gaze.

"What did I do?" The words spilled from my mouth. I expected the detective to accuse Kai, not this. Somewhere deep down, I hoped he wouldn't answer though—not in front of Wendy.

"Mommy, what's going on?" she asked.

He grunted as if in response to her. This wasn't the Detective Wilhelm I knew. At one time, he worked hard for justice. Last I'd worked with him, he'd grown lazy and out of shape. Now, he had the strength and physique of a much younger man. It felt unnatural coming from him, not unlike his strange behavior at the crime scene. When and why had he changed so much?

The handcuffs clicked, sealing shut around my wrists. When he gave them a tug to be sure they'd locked, it felt he'd pull my arms right off my body. My shoulders nearly yanked from their sockets at nothing but the flick of his wrist. His hot breath on my neck made my stomach curdle.

"Confess it now, Mari," he said, his voice rough. "Say it and maybe I'll let you off the hook."

Everything happened too fast. While I couldn't get over his surprising strength, he'd moved on to trying to force an admission of murder from me.

He squeezed my wrists tighter and I could have sworn my bones would crumble under his unnatural grip. Through the pain, his strength triggered the memory of the list I'd created in my mind's eye. *Story-book character determined by excessive strength and speed.*

A gasp escaped me but it wasn't because he barked another demand.

"Confess," he breathed.

I ignored him and raked through my thoughts to recall the rest of the list. Though we didn't have a lot of specifics, the clues were solid. *Murderer was a man. He followed me from the crime scene. Wore boots.*

Detective Wilhelm was the last person I'd ever have suspected, but with his odd behavior the day of the murder coupled with the other clues, I couldn't ignore the thought. A lump gathered in my throat.

"I don't know what you're talking about," I said between clenched teeth.

He laughed without joy. "Yes, you do. You've interfered with an investigation for your own gain."

What he said was right, but I couldn't confess with Wendy watching. She'd already lost her daddy. Hearing her mommy admit to a crime was too much.

Detective Wilhelm tugged on my arms. The angle with which they twisted sent aching jolts through my elbows and the cuffs squeezed my wrists too tightly.

"Say I'm right," he barked.

I seethed as he yanked again. Suddenly my stomach iced over. Frost spread from my womb up into my ribcage. It seemed the cold stopped my heart and my lungs froze over. The iciness crawled over my legs. Like a frozen lake, the skin on my arms cracked with the sound of ice splitting. I only registered the pain of the detective's grip and where the scab on my earlobe had ripped open, fresh and bleeding again—or so I guess based on the trickle of liquid down the side of my neck.

"What the hell?" The detective suddenly released his grasp on my arms.

The handcuffs froze. Ice fractured the metal, and the cuffs split open. They clattered to the ground. I twisted to see it with my own eyes. The magic from the child inside my body had indeed split cracks through solid metal.

"It's like Queen Elsa with her snow powers," Wendy said, voice at a whisper. She stared up at me in awe.

It's not me. Jack lodged his foot against my belly button as if trying to fight the detective from within. Was he protecting me? My son's magic sent shivers down my spine as admiration and a slice of fear struck me.

Free now, I eased off the wall. The iciness melted away and my body returned to normal.

Detective Wilhelm glared at Wendy. "What did you say?"

She only blinked at him in a moment of silence while her gaze raked over his face, then darted away. "You don't look like a person."

Red washed over the detective's neck and he narrowed his eyes at her. He snapped his attention from her in a flash and beckoned for me to step away from the wall. With two fingers, he instructed me where to stand. After Jack's icy protest, the detective kept his distance.

The chain of the handcuffs crunched under his feet as he stepped back. He released a curse and stooped to retrieve them from beneath the thick sole of his boot.

Why hadn't I put the clues together before? He always wore hideous hiking boots despite how poorly they matched his more professional attire.

He shoved the handcuffs in the pocket of his long coat. "Cuffs or not," he said. "Mari Rowan, you're under arrest for aiding and abetting in the murder of Christa Lang."

Another gasp. This time I spotted the source. Tala stared at me along with Scarlet and Wendy. Was Wilhelm's voice the same one Tala had heard the morning of the Snow Queen's murder?

"Come without a fight and you'll be doing yourself a favor," he said.

I had no other choice but to obey. Besides, I wanted to talk with Detective Wilhelm alone. At the station, I might glean information about his involvement—if any. Was it too crazy to consider him a suspect? He'd acted weird at the crime scene when he listened to Reese and me. A man, taller than Christa who stood at a model's height, attacked her and likely me, too. He fit the description and he knew where to find the murder weapon. But why follow me to the park? Why knock me out? What did he really want from me?

"I need shoes," I said. At least this, he allowed me to do. I stepped inside and gave Wendy a quick kiss on the head. Bending over took too much effort, so I shoved my wide feet into a pair of slip-on shoes.

Before I turned toward the staircase at the end of the hall, I locked eyes with Scarlet. As discreet as possible, I signaled her with a slight nod toward the detective's feet.

Are you thinking what I'm thinking?

The skin on her face tightened as her eyebrows lifted. Recognition dawned in her green eyes like sunlight in a forest. Scar returned the gesture with a lift of her chin.

After a quick glance, I confirmed Detective Wilhelm didn't notice our exchange. I scanned his scowling face and caught a hint of something bright in his eyes. Was it confidence? If he'd killed Christa, was this arrest to keep me from finding the truth?

I frowned as he met my gaze.

What's your motive for murder, detective?

Chapter Twelve

"There is nothing more deceptive than an obvious fact."

— Arthur Conan Doyle

The cold metal of the table between us dug into my swollen belly. After a night spent on the hard cot in the holding cell, every joint in my body screamed. The bright light of the interrogation room's fluorescent bulb forced me to squint.

Despite the early hour of the morning, Detective Wilhelm had arrived bright-eyed and bushy-tailed. To add to my shock, he didn't even have a greasy breakfast sandwich in hand or coffee on his breath. The intensity in his gaze and energy behind his words didn't match the man I'd worked alongside for so many years.

I shifted my body weight back as far as I could to take the pressure off of my legs. With a quick glance at my feet to make sure they were still there, I noted the fluid in my feet. I felt nothing below my knees and stretching my legs didn't get enough blood flowing there.

"What are you doing?" Detective Wilhelm asked. The slap of his palm against the tabletop caused me to flinch. Normally, his gruff behavior only earned him a glare from me, but today was different. Today, I sat across from a murderer.

I swallowed the gasp caught in my throat. "I'm too big for this chair."

He snorted and raked his judgmental gaze over my pregnant stomach. "You'd better get used to a little discomfort. Where you're going, they don't let women have drugs during birth."

I couldn't stop my face from twisting at the thought of that pain. What would it be like to deliver the embodiment of winter?

"That's right." Detective Wilhelm mistook my unpleasant expression as proof that I believed him.

That's wrong, actually. Instead of arguing about childbirth, something of which this creep knew nothing about, I bit my tongue.

He kicked his chair back and settled comfortably with his legs stretched and arms folded across his chest. "*Now* are you ready to say yes?"

I opened my mouth but clamped it shut again before saying something I'd regret. Not only did I need to avoid incriminating myself, but if I played the conversation right, I could glean information from him.

I didn't have a solid case against him, yet. A few matched descriptions didn't prove him involved, especially when it seemed he had no connection to the victim. But the feeling that nagged at me told me enough.

"What do you mean?" I asked, carefully.

He forced air through his nose and shook his head. "Confess. Say *yes, you're right, Wilhelm.*"

The fact that he didn't ask for admission of the crime itself struck me as odd. I filed the thought away into an imaginary red folder. Unfortunately, the organization cabinet in my mind's eye was already crammed with too many urgent notices.

"No," I snapped. Anger twisted my tone of voice when I'd meant to stay calm.

Ebenezer Scrooge. I silently cursed at myself for letting the detective get the best of me. If only I had the hood, I'd confirm his status as a storybook character and I could continue the case from there. Wild theories in moments of desperation didn't bode well for those who collected problems, like me. I needed to screw my head on straight, pregnancy brain or not, and organize my thoughts. Of course, no matter how color-coordinated, minimal clues didn't solve Christa's murder. Proof did. Confession did.

"Come on, Mari," he said. "Say yes." The impatience in his voice set me on edge. This new version of Detective Wilhelm was unpredictable. I never thought I'd miss the sexist, Taco Bell-obsessed side of him. At one time, I could guess what he'd say before it came out of his mouth. He'd joke about my physical weakness as a woman or grunt his appreciation whenever I helped solve a case.

He sat up and placed both palms flat on the table, leaning closer to me. "Do I have to force it out of you?"

Another shiver. Quickly, I gave my belly a gentle rub before Jack could react. If my son intended to defend me with his magic, it could trigger more aggression from the detective. Wilhelm could accuse me of not cooperating and slap me with an extra criminal charge or two. It was only us in the quiet, empty interrogation room with no witnesses.

"How about this? If you help me, I'll help you," he said. "We'll make a simple trade, but I have to hear you say it."

"What?"

"*Yes.*"

Where did his weird obsession with my agreeability come from? He should be curating a confession from me if he wanted to close this case—not beating around the bush.

"What would my motive be?" I asked.

"That she threatened—" he groaned, interrupting himself. After rubbing his eyes, he cleared his throat and started again. "Maybe you just didn't like what she had to say about your baby."

Absentmindedly, I rubbed my stomach again. How did he know? Christa died and the only other person who'd witnessed her threat was Kai. Unless she spoke with the detective before he killed her. The questions only circled back to one important mystery: what was Detective Wilhelm's motive for murder?

"Actually, she told me exactly what I wanted to hear about my pregnancy." I spoke the truth. "You can call all my past doctors and confirm that they didn't believe I was with child. She did, which means I had no reason to hurt her."

"Then work with me," he said, fixing his intense gaze on me. The darkness in his eyes twisted my stomach. "You know something I don't, and all I'm asking for is access to that. Deal?"

Did he want me to admit that Kai was there? If Wilhelm killed her, what would this admission gain?

My heart skipped a beat. *I can't let him frame Kai.*

"No," I answered. I'd never let him or anyone else call my husband a murderer.

He forced a breath through his nose and knocked his knuckles against the table. The disturbing smile that spread across his face held no joy. He kicked the chair back from the table and stood.

"I'm sick of this!" he shouted. When his fist slammed against the table, a yelp escaped me. The metal dented under the force of the impact.

Before I could dodge his grasp, he reached across the table and closed his fingers around my forearm.

Jack reacted. Just as before, the iciness started from within my womb. Frost spread to my extremities faster this time, but the detective didn't let go. Instead, he squeezed tighter as he stepped to the side of the table and pulled me from the chair.

"I'm done waiting for permission," he said.

"You're hurting me." I tried to wrench away from his grasp but it only triggered more aggression. He threw me toward the door. My foot caught on the table's leg and the gray linoleum came up faster than I could react.

Instinct sent my hands out, but not in time. My wrists and elbows took the brunt of the fall. Thankfully, Jack sensed the change in balance and the weight of his body vanished entirely. He'd gone from using his magic for defense to shifting into frost.

Heavy boots landed inches from my head. My chin grazed the linoleum as I looked up at the toe of his shoes in front of me.

"Get up," he said.

Small stains dotted the front of his boots. Speckles of dark red ruined the smooth tan surface. *Proof.*

I pulled my knees underneath me and pushed up, craning my neck to see his face. "Why did you kill her?"

He laughed.

"There's blood, on your shoes. It's Christa's isn't it?" I said.

"We're leaving," he said, taking a step back. "Get up."

Slowly, I pushed to my feet. I carefully rolled my wrists to make sure the fall hadn't caused a sprain. The surface pain signaled that bruises would appear soon.

"Why did you kill her?" I asked.

"You're going to do what I say," he ignored the question.

Detective Wilhelm had one hand on the door handle and the other inside his jacket. Based on the angle, he was reaching for the weapon in his holster. Apparently, bruised wrists were the least of my worries. Did he really think he needed a gun against a waddling pregnant woman?

He frowned when he noticed my gaze shift to the door beside him. If I raised my voice, someone in the station might hear my accusation. The interrogation room was in the back corner, and everyone knew Detective Wilhelm got away with working alone, but I was within arm's length of the door. I wouldn't win in a race or a wrestle to get through the door, but the chances of another officer hearing our struggle would help.

"What do you want me to do?" I asked.

He beckoned for me to step in front of him with two fingers. As if I was an airplane preparing to land, he pointed where I should stand. When I didn't move, he pulled the gun from his side and waved it toward the door.

"I'm not letting you frame me for the murder you committed," I spoke carefully, keeping my eye on his weapon. The safety was off and his finger hovered the trigger. I stood right in front of him but he didn't aim it directly at me. Instead, the barrel pointed at the space between me and my escape. If he wanted to kill me, he'd hold it up, directed between my eyes.

"Let's go," he growled.

Memories of Jameson, the wolf, flooded me. He was a rough man, an obvious choice for the story aura to give him a villain's role. While Detective Wilhelm had plenty of his own distasteful traits, I couldn't pin which story he'd come from.

Was he a true villain or a vague antagonist like the Snow Queen? And why frame me for her murder? How did that fit into a story's plot? What classic book told the tale of a man using an innocent woman to cover his crime?

If I ever got out of this interrogation room, I had hours of research ahead of me. At least it'd help me keep my promise to take Wendy to the library.

I finally tore my eyes from the gun and met his gaze. "If you're taking me to sign a confession, I won't do it."

He raised the barrel, aiming for the soft spot of my throat. "I didn't want to have to threaten you. It's so much more satisfying to play with people."

Ew. What in the wonderland did that mean? *Villain.* He was definitely a villain.

"But I'm done waiting," he continued. With his free hand, he grabbed my aching wrist and forced me to turn. "Open the door." The hard metal tip of the gun dug into my ribcage. He tugged the thick fabric of my hoodie away from my body, likely to conceal the weapon.

I did as he said, reaching for the door handle and twisting. For him, it'd appear as though I obeyed. For me, I wanted to close the distance between us and the rest of the precinct. Safety in numbers always helped.

Thanks, mom. When we stepped out of the room, I recalled my mother's warnings to never go out alone. She'd raised me to be aware and cautious, though I'd broken her safety rules many times lately. And, of course, it'd earned me a punch to the face—worse, if Scarlet and Reese hadn't arrived in time.

With every step I took through the maze of offices and desks, another piece of the puzzle formed in my mind's eye.

We had the trail of clues that showed Wilhelm had followed me to

Pioneer Park. Had *he* tampered with the hood? It didn't make sense. If he was a character in a story, he'd follow the plot just as Kai had—leaving with the Snow Queen into the winter weather.

I tensed as he pressed the gun harder against my ribs. As we weaved through the precinct, I realized he was guiding me to the front door. Instead of signing a confession, he was taking me outside.

The bastard knows about the rift. Detective Wilhelm didn't want to frame me for murder, he wanted power. Or so I guessed, based on what I knew of him. The desire for control matched his overbearing personality.

Did he want story magic? Or the hood itself? Either way, he was a murderer, and I couldn't give a killer that kind of power.

I stopped in my tracks, halfway between the front desk and the sliding double doors.

"What are you doing?" He breathed into my ear and jabbed the gun into me. If he pushed any harder, he might break my rib. The intent of the gesture was a reminder of his threat.

Slowly, frost spread. Jack clearly didn't like the creep hurting his mommy, again.

I felt like Elsa in *Frozen*, walking to her coronation with ice threatening to expose itself on her skin. But I wasn't the one with something to hide.

I tilted my chin back, watching the reflection of the precinct in the glass doors. The officer at the front desk was busy with a phone at one ear and her hand's on the computer's keyboard.

"You won't kill me," I whispered.

"Walk."

"If you were going to shoot me, you would have done it in the back where the walls are soundproof. You need me alive."

The harsh scrape of his teeth gritting together caused me to cringe. I flinched and the crackle of ice split down my arms and over my fingertips. If I was wrong, and the detective risked it all to kill me right here in the middle of the police station, would the ice save my life? Could Jack's powers block a bullet?

I didn't want to find out, but I held my ground, confident I had the upper hand. The fact that I'd told him I had proof he'd murdered Christa only solidified my theory that he would have already shot me if he didn't need me.

"I won't do what you want, I can promise that right now. Let me walk out of here and I won't tell this whole precinct about the blood on your shoes."

The pressure from the hard barrel didn't let up. It seemed he held his breath while deciding. The hot air that had brushed against my frozen neck ceased.

You need me. I repeated silently. I clung to the hope that he wouldn't end it all right now out of sheer impatience and frustration. Now it was me who didn't breathe.

I felt nothing, not the beat of my pulse nor the throbbing ache in my wrists. My hands had nearly turned to solid ice. The option to obey the detective's command was gone now. I was frozen in place, a human statue, unable to even blink.

Finally, the frost dissipated twice as fast as it came. My heart resumed its rhythmic thud in my chest. I flexed my fingers first and noticed the weapon was no longer jammed between my spine and ribcage.

"This isn't over," he said. "You have one day. No funny business and no bargaining. Meet me at Pioneer Park at sunrise tomorrow or your husband dies."

Everything inside of me melted at once, turning from ice to sludge. My entire body felt sick with aches, nausea, and all-encompassing fear.

He has Kai.

Now that I registered the existence of my limbs again, I shuffled my feet. I turned to face the harsh gaze of the detective—the unnamed villain.

"Who are you?"

Instead of answering, Detective Wilhelm shoved past me. The doors slid open at the weight of his approaching steps. Snowflakes swirled in a flurry and then settled on the floor inside the door. They promptly melted.

Beyond the sliding doors, the sheen of the icy concrete glistened in the sunshine. Winter had cracked, and I almost felt the warmth of summer coming.

The detective's bloody speckled boot slammed against the sidewalk, shattering my fantasy. When he stepped outside, he tucked his hands into his coat's pockets and took a sharp turn to the right.

For now, I stood victorious as he made good on the deal to let me walk away. A weight pressed on my chest and it wasn't Jack's foot against my sternum.

Although I no longer had a gun on me, nothing about this felt like a win.

Chapter Thirteen

"Everything you look at can become a fairy tale and you can get a story from everything you touch."

— Hans Christian Andersen

City sounds permeated my thoughts. Each siren, honking horn, or pedestrian shout made me flinch. With the sun's return, people took to the streets again. Though it was still cold with sporadic snow flurries, the sun had invited Saturday shoppers and brunchers outside. What would it feel like to wander through the weekend without a care in the world?

The swelling in my ankles and ache in my feet had me moving slower with each step. While the timeline pushed me to walk faster, the threat at the end nearly kept me paralyzed. The result was a dazed shuffle. I wandered the streets without a destination, and without a plan.

What did Detective Wilhelm want with Storyland? Magic? Power? Since he'd become a villain, though I had yet to identify which one, I couldn't give him any such access. Wilhelm had succumbed to the unforgivable act of murder which earned him the role of an evil antagonist in both real life and the fictional.

I dragged one foot in front of the other, scraping the heels of my slip-on shoes against the concrete. Morning traffic filled the air with exhaust. Pure white snowflakes sliced through puffs of pollution like bullets cutting into flesh.

I weaved past pedestrians, avoiding a group of women who carried their heeled sandals. Their walk of shame had nothing on mine. I'd gotten myself framed for murder and manipulated by the detective on the case.

I kept my head down and dodged a jogger who ran up the slanted sidewalk. Saturday mornings were a combination of hungover college kids, runners, middle-aged brunchers, and me. If only I had a plan for the day like everyone I passed.

With only twenty-four hours to respond to the detective's demand, I wanted to give up. If I threw in the towel and gave him whatever he wanted, my husband would live. Or, I could predict Wilhelm's intention based on the plot his story and try to get a step ahead of him. This was no different from other fairy tales I'd twisted or sealed to save lives—except that two years had passed and I'd become rustier than a nail left out in the rain.

I finally stopped wandering and decided it was time to call Scarlet. Habit had me reaching in my back pocket for my phone. I sighed when I felt nothing but the worn fabric of the old jeans against my hands. I'd forgotten everything at the police station except for the clothes on my back.

I shoved my hands into the hoodie's front pocket. Finally, I looked at my surroundings. To my right, a tall stone building towered over me. The glow of warm lights filled the windows and hope immediately washed over me.

Despite my daze, I'd found myself in front of the public library. Renewed energy carried me up the concrete steps and through the doors. Rows of books and the faint smell of coffee welcomed me. The rushed, chaotic sounds of the city muted as the door shut behind me.

The quiet calm of readers and hushed whispers cleared my head. I returned the librarian's smile as I passed the front desk. The woman pushed her thin glasses higher on her nose and offered me a kind nod.

I located the public phones and dialed. My heart leaped when Kai's voice came through the other line. Without thinking, I'd punched in his number. His answering message ended, followed by a short beep.

"I miss you," I said. Of course, nobody would receive the message.

My throat squeezed as I ended the call and dialed Scarlet's number. Unlike most modern people, she didn't have an aversion to answering the call of an unknown number. We shared mutual relief at the sound of one another's voices. I explained the situation as quickly as possible.

"I'm so glad he let you go," she said.

"Scar, I think Detective Wilhelm wants power, or maybe the hood."

"Those are the same thing. And you can't give it to him."

Couldn't I? If it'd spare the life of the man I loved, wasn't one villain's immortality or magic worth it? I bit my tongue.

"Mari?" she said after a moment of silence. "You won't give him the hood, right?"

"Right," I muttered.

"Nothing good can come from it. He's already a judgmental, greedy person—a *killer*."

So were you. I opened my mouth but stopped myself before giving the words life. Scarlet wasn't cold-blooded, just desperate to keep the magic of fiction from destroying our world.

After she agreed to meet me here with Wendy, I hung up and found a round table in the back corner. Among the shadows of the tall bookshelves, I claimed the empty table with my hoodie slung over the back of the chair. The cold didn't bother me, anyway.

I waddled through the aisles, gathering an armful of fairy tales and classic books. Different editions offered slight variations in the narrative. The differences in each story might trigger answers about Detective Wilhelm's identity. I grabbed everything Hans Christian Andersen had ever published. I figured the same author as Christa's tale was the best place to start.

The stack in my arms teetered like a tower of Jenga blocks. I shuffled slowly back to the table and eased into the squeaky seat. I slid the stack onto the table and started with the book on top and then worked my way down.

Beautiful illustrations of *Thumbelina*, *The Emperor's New Clothes*, and *The Princess and the Pea* consumed the next thirty minutes.

"Mommy!"

I looked up, rubbing visions of tiny fairies and sleeping princesses from my eyes. My own tiny fairy bounded in my direction, complete with a bouncing messy ponytail. Of course, Wendy wasn't really the fairy in her tale. Instead of Tinker Bell, the story aura selected her for the role of Peter Pan. Unfortunately, it suited her in that she was fiercely independent, fearless, and overconfident, which had gotten her into trouble more than a few times.

Wendy dodged a college guy who backed his chair into her path. She skipped toward the back corner and threw her arms around my neck. The book of collected Andersen tales fell from my hands as I returned her hug.

I patted down her wild, escaped hairs from the loose ponytail. It appeared Auntie Scar had tried her best with Wendy's hair. After hundreds of years with perfect curls that belonged to an immortal body, Scarlet never learned to use a brush.

Books on the other hand, were her second nature. Scarlet stooped to pick up the fallen tale and return it to the stack.

"Any luck?" she asked, brows furrowed.

I shook my head. "What about you?"

Curls cascaded over her shoulder at the sharp turn of her head. Scarlet's gaze raked over the shelf marked *fairy tales*. She worked her tongue in her mouth. "No. Still a starving witch, I guess."

"If I had the hood, I'd be able to identify you," I said. Why did I feel the need to convince her? I was the Keeper of Stories. It was *my* hood. And *my* husband's life was on the line, not hers.

Wendy grabbed *The Little Mermaid* from the middle of the stack and flipped it open. With her knees on the chair, she propped herself over the book and looked immersed with each page she turned.

Finally, Scarlet broke her gaze on the bookshelf behind me and scanned the stack I'd gathered. "Why only Andersen?" she asked. "With the rip in the rift, Wilhelm could be anyone."

She marched past my chair and started building her own tower of tales. At this rate, we might as well tilt the whole fairy tale shelf and dump every book. I pictured myself diving into the imaginary pile like a child jumping among leaves. The image of so many books sent my heart to the depths of my stomach. There simply wasn't enough time to study every classic character ever written.

After another two hours slipped by, we'd scanned the pages of dozens of fairy tales and classic books. The illustrations, texts, and titles all mixed like alphabet soup in my memory. Nothing stuck out as a definite representation of the detective's behavior.

I sighed and slumped forward. "Wilhelm could be anyone," I repeated, as my gaze swept over the stacks of hardback covers, "from Moriarty to that monster, thing in *Beowulf*." I waved my hand at the pile of books.

"Moriarty isn't a bad guess," Scarlet said. She plopped into the seat across from me. The stack in her arms tumbled onto the table like dominos, one by one. "But does Detective Wilhelm really have extreme intelligence?"

"Hmm." I nodded, understanding her implication. I eyed Scarlet's selection, giving her a pointed to look when she opened *Little Brother and Little Sister*. As far as I knew, that was another title for *Hansel and Gretel*. Why didn't Scarlet believe that she wasn't the evil witch? Other stories had hunger as the theme or a plot point. Not to mention the crucial fact that the story aura still only landed on people who matched the character.

My stomach grumbled—a reminder that I hadn't eaten since the two bites of breakfast in the holding cell.

Hunger...I rolled the word over in my mind. It stuck out to me as if written in bold, red letters. *The Gingerbread Man*? No, now I was just thinking about cookies.

"What about the story where the character craves radishes, or something, from the garden next door?"

"What?" Scarlet arched her eyebrow, annoyed at my interruption.

"Your tale," I said. "Or did I confuse that with *Peter Rabbit*?"

"I'm not a rabbit," she said, nose in the air. "But I do have a craving."

"From a garden?"

A faraway look glazed over her eyes. "Yeah." She blinked and met my gaze. "Let's focus on the detective's character instead."

I nodded. I knew I needed to focus on the detective's character, not Scarlet's, but the pull of getting close to answers intoxicated me. It felt we'd reached the tipping point with her tale, but barely scratched the surface of the detective's story.

Wendy slapped *The Little Mermaid* shut and pushed it to the side. Her tongue curled at the edge of her mouth as she stretched as far as she could to reach across the table and see the pictures in the book Scarlet had opened.

"I have no idea where Wilhelm belongs," I said. After hours without food, a miserable night, a morning of the detective's verbal—and physical—attacks, and then a threat to my husband's life, I was done. So overdone, in fact, that I felt like a beached whale baking in the sun on the shore. I ran my hand over the top of my stomach.

"I do," Scarlet said. As soon as she abandoned the book she'd selected for a new one, Wendy stole it out from underneath her. Scarlet reached across the table and pushed *The Snow Queen* from the stack. Quickly, she caught the two books on top of it before they tumbled to the table and suffered dented spines or bent edges. "Go back to the source."

I groaned and slid the book closer to me. The Snow Queen's icy gaze stared back at me.

"I've already tried to place him. There are too many characters—"

"It's a picture of daddy!" Wendy interrupted. She jabbed her finger against the pages of the open book in front of her.

Library patrons glanced at our not-so-quiet corner. The excitement in Wendy's 'outside voice' turned more than a few heads. Scarlet and I exchanged a look and leaned forward at the same time. As we scanned the book in front of Wendy, breath caught in my throat.

A black and white illustration of *Little Brother and Little Sister* filled a page opposite the text of the story. While the girl had run ahead, the boy was glancing back at the viewer. He left a trail of bread-crumbs alongside his footsteps.

My eyes glued to the drawing of Hansel where Wendy's little finger pointed.

"What do you mean, Wednesday?" I asked, calling her by the nickname Kai had created for her.

"This looks like daddy the day he went on his trip," she said.

Scarlet and I exchanged furrowed brows.

"Like a little boy?" I asked.

When she shook her head, more hair escaped her messy ponytail. "Like his face."

The explanation didn't make sense. Kai looked nothing like the curly-haired, bony child in the illustration. Still something about this clue made sense.

Hannibal...Kai's queue clued me in on a connection. The witch ate humans and so did the serial killer in the TV show he'd saved but would never watch. If the restaurant was acknowledging his status as the boy Kai, could the *Hannibal* selection point to the cannibalistic nature of *Little Brother and Little Sister*?

My gaze shifted from the drawing of Hansel to the *Snow Queen*'s pages in front of me.

Scarlet yanked the book out from under my elbows. She flipped to the middle and located a picture of the boy Kai. In the drawing, he sat on his knees in front of the Snow Queen's throne. Around them, a vast frozen lake spread for as far as the eye could see.

Before Scarlet even pointed to the boy, Wendy perked up. She shifted from her knees to her feet and perched in a crouched position in the squeaky chair.

"That's what he looked like when you told me I was going to have a baby brother or sister," she said. Enormous eyes full of confidence and curiosity stared up at me. A sigh escaped her and her shoulders slumped. "I miss Daddy."

My heart cracked but Scarlet gave neither of us time to grieve.

"It's like with Alistair," she said, breathless. Clearly, her mind worked faster than mine. While she turned to Wendy, I turned the thought over in my mind. What had Wendy said about Christa's boyfriend? "Wendy, the man we spoke with at the fancy apartment—"

"The hairy guy?" she asked.

Hairy? Was that how she saw him? Alistair was all muscle and glistening skin. Either he'd shaved his chest or was naturally hairless across his body—the opposite of whatever Wendy saw.

Again, Scarlet looked at me with wide eyes. "I guess," she said. "Did he look different to you? Maybe like someone you've seen in a movie or book?"

Wendy shrugged. "I think so. Some people don't even look like people."

What she said didn't sound possible, but everything about Storyland's influence over our world had changed. I reached out and ran my palm over the back of her head, smoothing the flyaways of her messy hair. A flutter of rapid beats tightened my chest and a sharp pain shot through my heart. Never had I wanted to drag my daughter—my children—into this life. Despite my best efforts to keep Wendy's childhood normal and my pregnancy with Jack healthy, both had found themselves entangled with stories.

"Why didn't you tell me?" I asked. "Can you see glowing colors around people?"

"When did this start?" Scarlet joined in.

Poor Wendy flipped her head back and forth to acknowledge both of us. The questions came too fast. Instead of answering, she squeezed her eyes shut and hid her face in her palms.

I scooted my chair closer to hers and pulled her into a side hug. "I'm sorry. That was too much."

"It's okay." She shrugged and emerged from her shell at my comforting touch. "I kind of like what I see. It's like watching TV all the time." A cheeky grin spread across her rosy face. She'd yet to remove her puffy, marshmallow jacket since the library was drafty. Now, the warmth of energy and excitement from our interest had her cheeks turning pink.

The earlier fear melted, and I shared a dash of that excitement. If she wasn't afraid, I wouldn't be the one to instill thoughts of worry. Instead, maybe her newfound power could be the answer to subverting Wilhelm's threat.

"And it looks like magic when people change," she said, beaming. The confident smile reminded me of the character she'd become.

I cleared my throat and spoke in a quiet voice. "Wendy, has your face ever changed?"

When she nodded, eyes bright and full of energy, it confirmed my suspicions.

Wendy can see the story aura. But how? The hood materialized in my mind's eye. If I'd worn it while pregnant with her, I'd consider the possibility that I'd passed its powers to her. That theory fell flat since I'd given birth to her before I even knew living fairy tales existed.

"Yep, I have magic too." She stretched her legs, standing from her crouched position. Like Peter, she stood atop her chair with fists on her hips and feet pointed out. "Even when I'm not smiling, it still looks like I'm smiling."

Peter Pan's mischievous smirk popped into my mind's eye. How and when had this all evolved? A million questions flooded me but I forced myself to keep quiet and not inundate my daughter. How this new magic had developed, didn't matter at the moment. Right now, we had a timeline to save her father's life, and Wendy might answer the one question I'd been scraping for all day—the question that could change the course of Kai's fate.

Who was Detective Wilhelm?

Chapter Fourteen

"I have frequently gained my first real insight into the character of parents by studying their children."

— Arthur Conan Doyle

Before I could ask Wendy about the man who'd arrested me, Scarlet went into a panic. Her heavy breathing coupled with frantic movements and distracted me from the matter at hand. Could Kai be both Hansel and the boy from *The Snow Queen*? Did the hood's magic mess with the story aura that much?

As wild as it sounded, it made sense. Not only did it connect with the clue left in his TV queue, but it explained his mismatched behaviors.

Scarlet raised a finger, pulling me from my thoughts again.

"I need to know," she spoke through her teeth and tucked a curl behind her ear. In a flurry, she shuffled through the pages of *Little Brother and Little Sister*. I'd never seen her so careless with a book before. Once she found the snarling face of the evil witch, she turned the book around to show Wendy. "Is this me?"

Wendy frowned at the sight of the disturbing woman. The book depicted the witch with soulless black eyes and thin skin stretched over a cruel, twisted mouth. The way the frightening woman glared at the children on her doorstep soured my stomach.

My daughter's eyes widened before she quickly darted her gaze away. When she looked up, Scarlet was nearly foaming at the mouth.

Scarlet's chest heaved, and she licked her lips. Clearly, it took every ounce of restraint not to lunge across the table and shake the answer out of Wendy. I peaked an eyebrow at the former Keeper of Stories and scooted an inch closer to my daughter. Though I didn't believe Scarlet's character claim, I wasn't sure how well she'd take Wendy's response.

Finally, Wendy spoke. "You're not a witch, Auntie Scar. You're just really round."

A sudden giggle bubbled up inside of me. The answer was so unexpected, I couldn't stop the laugh that burst from me. The tension of Kai's disappearance and Christa's murder, not to mention my arrest, finally split—if just a sliver. Out came inappropriate relief as laughter. I curled my lips inward to keep from laughing too loudly. We'd already earned the sharp glare of too many people in the library.

Scarlet's jaw dropped, and she blinked, clearly struggling to process the information.

"Round?" she asked. The description didn't match the woman I saw. Since Scarlet had eaten little lately—always hungry but never satisfied—her cheeks had become gaunt and her arms bony.

"Yeah." Wendy held her arms out in front of torso as if showing us the size of a pizza. Her fingers linked and she froze in the pose on top of her chair. "But not as round as Mommy, so I guess your baby is not as chubby as my brother." With that, she hopped off the chair and plopped her rear end in the squeaky seat.

A baby? The bubble of laughter suddenly ceased, and the air seemed sucked from my lungs. When I tried to gasp, my throat felt too tight to inhale.

"My…what?" Scarlet breathed. "Am I?"

"The cravings," I whispered conspiratorially. "Which characters are pregnant?"

She shook her head. "I can't believe it."

The small smile that curled at the corners of her mouth betrayed her words. Clearly, she considered this good news. I could tell by the light that brightened her eyes that this was the best possible answer she could have imagined.

Suddenly, she slapped her hands against the table. A book that was teetering on the edge of the tower toppled over, falling open on its pages. I offered an apologetic smile to the college students who whipped their heads in our direction.

"I know who I am!" Scarlet squealed. Her eyes searched the stack of books until she found the right title and plucked it from the pile. "And there's a witch in the story, but it's not me." The hardcover of the book knocked against the table when she flipped it open. A gasp escaped her as she stared at the open pages. Slowly, she lifted the book. In gold letters the title scrawled across a green cover read *Rapunzel*.

She flipped it around and pointed to a man kneeling in flowers. A witch stood over him with arms crossed and an exaggerated grimace.

"This is Rampion, the plant that blooms Rapunzel flowers," Scarlet said with her finger on the tall white stalks with small purple petals. "This is what I'm craving. And this is Rapunzel's father making a deal with the witch who owns the garden. He's trading his daughter for access to the Rapunzel for his wife to eat."

"So you're—"

"Rapunzel's mother!" she shouted.

A college girl scoffed at the loud interruption but her friends laughed. I didn't blame them, considering Scarlet had just announced that she was pregnant with a fictional character. To those who'd overheard our conversation, we sounded deluded. Or perhaps they thought we'd fully committed to a roleplaying game.

Scarlet shot out of her seat and tucked the old copy of *Rapunzel* under her arm. "I'm sorry, I can't just sit here. Give me something to do. Let's kidnap Wilhelm or something."

I faked a laugh and glanced at the eavesdroppers. Hopefully, they didn't call the cops on us.

"We can't," I hissed. "It's too risky. If we mess with him, he could

—" I cut myself off and glanced at Wendy. She had her nose deep in *Little Brother and Little Sister*. Instead of saying the word aloud, I dragged my finger across my throat and made a small cutting sound. "So for Kai's safety, we're stuck."

Scarlet flipped her curls over her shoulders and straightened. With her chin in the air, she peered down her nose at me. "That's only if Detective Wilhelm is telling the truth."

"You think he's lying about Kai?"

"I think we have the upper hand." Her gaze shifted to Wendy. "Maybe Wilhelm is the witch."

"And Aunt Gerda is Gretel," Wendy added without looking up from the fairy tale.

No way. When I'd found Kai's phone and the clue buried inside, I was right to consider it a breadcrumb. Goosebumps prickled my neck and arms as another thought struck me. Gerda wasn't answering my calls because she, too, had been kidnapped. Was her note written by the same person who'd taken Kai?

Is Blair Danes the witch who wants to cook and eat them? My stomach curdled.

Casually, Wendy turned to the next page in the book and cocked her head at the illustration. "But the angry detective man doesn't look like the witch. So why are Daddy and Aunt Gerda the little boy and girl?"

"Who does he look like?" I asked.

My heart dropped when Wendy shrugged. "I don't know. He's scary, so I tried not to look at him for very long. But he's not the witch, I'm sure of it." She pointed between the soulless black eyes on the page. "The witch is a person and the angry man isn't."

Detective Wilhelm wasn't human. I'd already sealed Dracula's story and ended *Frankenstein*, so which monster could he be? Nothing about the new way the story magic behaved suggested the return of completed story plots. Besides, Wendy had seen Frankenstein's monster before and I was sure she'd have mentioned the evil vampire's fangs.

"Mari." Scarlet returned to her seat and leaned her elbows on the table. When she put too much weight on the table, it tipped toward her. I reached out and stopped the tower of tales from falling over. "That's a good thing. Wilhelm isn't the witch, but the witch is most likely the person who has Kai and Gerda. So that means he's bluffing."

I wanted to believe it. A speck of hope lifted my spirits. Maybe I didn't have to grant the detective—a villain—power or magic to save my husband's life.

"But we can't be sure," I said.

Scarlet licked her lips and then said, "not yet. But you're an investigator and he's a killer. What do you do when a suspect won't talk?"

I blinked, letting my gaze fall to where her hands were splayed on the table. If I put myself in the shoes I'd worn nearly a decade ago, before fairy tales and magic, I'd walk to the homes of witnesses or the suspect's family members. I frowned at the memory of the awful furry brown boots I used to wear.

"I'd interview others involved in the case," I said.

Scarlet smirked, her red lips tilted and eyes narrowed. "So we *can* be sure, if we find the witch."

It made sense. Identifying Wilhelm's character took too much time, and time was a luxury we didn't have. But we could still get ahead of him if we called his bluff. If I found the witch, I'd find Kai and his sister, ensure their safety, and then turn Wilhelm over to the authorities for killing Christa. This plan allowed us to keep story magic, or whatever power he sought from the rift or hood, out of the detective's hands.

I mirrored Scarlet's smile until Wendy poked her way through our locked gaze. She'd climbed onto the chair again and perched with her feet on the seat. Like us, she smiled mischievously.

No way was I letting my daughter anywhere near a child-eating witch. I opened my mouth, but Wendy spoke before I could.

"Can we get McDonald's?" she asked.

"Uh." I glanced at Wendy then back to Scarlet. "Do you think you could…?"

Scarlet nodded. "Yep." She stood and patted Wendy's back. "You hunt the witch while we get a snack."

"Yay!" Wendy hopped off the chair and jumped up and down beside Scarlet.

Now the college girls stared at us blatantly. They no longer tried to stifle their giggles or hide the shock on their faces. All five of them had twisted in their seats to watch us. This was beginning to feel like a reality TV show. *Survivor: Fairy Tale Edition.*

"Not McDonald's," Scarlet said, "but you can pick out chips from the drugstore." Then, with a wink at me, she spoke again. Her voice was too loud, but in typical Scarlet fashion, she didn't care what others thought. "I need to grab a little pregnancy test. And you—" she pointed at her eyes with two fingers then to the copy of *Little Brother and Little Sister.* "You will find the cannibal before she eats anyone."

Ew. I'd tried to avoid that thought. Hushed whispers came from the college girls as they peered at us and exchanged theories.

"Call me with the results of the test," I said.

"Got it." Scarlet threw me a thumbs up.

The thought of being pregnant at the same time as Scarlet almost made me giddy…If I had the energy for giddiness. In a normal life, I'd throw her a baby shower, and we'd raise our children as best friends—Jack Frost and Rapunzel, two peas in a fairytale pod.

It warmed my heart which apparently triggered Jack into a more solid existence. The weight of his body pressed against my pelvic bone. In the past couple of hours he'd shifted lower in my torso, pushing down as if he was finally ready to make his earthly debut.

I'm so tired of being pregnant, but now's not the time. I brushed my palm over my bulbous stomach. Hopefully, my water wouldn't break before I solved this case.

"Bye, Mommy." Wendy threw her arms around me. After a quick hug, she weaved through the maze of tables to catch up with Scarlet who'd headed for the exit. The librarian eyed them as they passed by and told Wendy not to run.

All at once, I was alone in the shadowy corner of the library again. But now I was armed with an arsenal of information.

"Yeah," I whispered. "I'll find the witch."

Blair Danes. The woman who'd supposedly witnessed Kai kill

Christa had to be the same person who'd taken him. I'd yet to find a connection between Christa and Detective Wilhelm, but what about a link from Christa to the witch?

Maybe Blair had interacted with the Snow Queen before. Maybe they were even friends like the group of girls who'd finally stopped staring at me. And if so, I knew just the man to ask.

I stood, grabbed *Little Brother and Little Sister* off the table, and marched to the front desk. I needed to pay Alistair a visit, and I planned to bring illustrated evidence of the witness.

Chapter Fifteen

"Where there is no imagination there is no horror."

— Arthur Conan Doyle

The walk to Alistair's neighborhood took too long. *Everything takes too long when your husband's life is on the line*. If I'd hailed a cab or booked an Uber, I'd be stuck in Saturday tourist traffic. But waddling several blocks wasn't ideal either.

None of the options got me from point A to point B fast enough, so I selected the one that gave me the most control. Besides, I didn't have a phone to call for a car or money to pay the driver.

With each step, Jack pressed lower. I cupped my stomach and refused to slow my pace. The closer I got to Alistair's side of town, the shorter the buildings became. The busy area around where restaurants lined every corner and the sidewalks teemed with pedestrians, faded behind me. Sounds of sirens were quieter and in the distance. In the residential zone of the wealthy, car engines didn't drown the sound of the waves off the San Francisco shore.

I inhaled the scent of sea salt. The refreshing sting wasn't as strong as normal. The thin blanket of snowflakes that decorated the concrete, and every windowsill suffocated the ocean's aroma. I'd grown tired of the plain, unassuming smell of snow. Thankfully, the winter's strength was waning, slowly but surely. For now, pedestrians still bundled in thick jackets and the white layer of snow coated the city like icing on a sugar cookie.

I longed for a warm cookie in the shape of a Christmas tree or candy cane. The constant winter had me in a holiday state of mind. But it was the focus on family, the quiet moments with my daughter and my husband that I truly wanted.

Even with Kai's occasional grumpy attitude or bitter behavior brought on by the shards of glass from the troll mirror, we'd enjoyed a cozy Christmas last year. Memories of Kai's smile, the warm sound of his laugh, and plenty of teasing between us, flooded me.

He'd tossed a pillow at me when he'd unwrapped the book of dad jokes. When I'd gushed over the locket he'd given me, he'd pulled me in for a tender hug. Emotion had taken me over at the sight of the empty side of the locket, the spot where our second child's photo would be placed. Tears had filled my eyes and had streaked my cheeks and my husband had kissed them away right there in front of the twinkling lights of the Christmas tree.

"I miss you, Kai," I whispered. My warm breath clashed with the chilly air in a swirl of white.

I reached for the locket at my throat. My fingers only found flesh and the thready beat of my pulse at the soft spot of my neck. My heart dropped when I remembered the sentimental piece of jewelry was still at the police station with the rest of my daily belongings.

Before I knew it, I stood at Alistair's doorstep and had to wipe the wetness from my eyes. I took a long breath, steadied myself, and knocked.

When the door swung open, thick heat washed over me. The humid air drifted from inside his home gym and I cringed for the sake of the books. He needed a good librarian to save his library from curled pages, warping, and mold growth.

"You again?" he huffed. Alistair sniffed and used the back of his forearm to wipe sweat from his temple. In his other hand, he gripped a seventy-pound kettlebell.

"Are you always exercising?" I asked. It was more a thought that slipped through than an actual question. Exhaustion and stress squelched my patience for polite behavior. And maybe I was a little envious of Alistair's simple life. If only my days were free to do with as I pleased. Though working out still wouldn't make the top of my list, unless putting on yoga pants counted as exercise.

He grunted as he hoisted the weight to his shoulder. After pausing for a moment and a slight bend in his knees, he hefted it straight up. "Keeps me in check," he said as he continued his workout. He repeated the movement, bringing the weight to his shoulder and then thrusting it above him again.

I arched my eyebrow and then gave my head a little shake. I pulled the book from beneath my arm and flipped through the pages.

Alistair cursed. "I guess I shouldn't say things like that to a cop."

"I'm not a cop," I said. "I'm an investigator."

He shrugged the side not holding the kettlebell. "Cop or not, I don't want anyone to think I hurt Christa." His eyes darted back and forth. He scanned the sidewalk with a frown twisting his mouth.

Alistair's obvious nerves would have raised suspicions if his alibi wasn't as solid as his abs. Besides, his agitation with Detective Wilhelm had been genuine—they definitely weren't working together. Still, I noted his behavior and filed it away for later research. What had Wendy said about him?

Yeah, no, he's absolutely not hairy. The sight of his bare, glistening chest confirmed I saw a different person than Wendy had witnessed. Alistair was a character, but not one I had time to dig into right now.

"Christa is who I came here to talk about. Well, her friends," I said. "Did she have any? Maybe a woman named Blair Danes?"

Alistair's brow flickered. Slowly, he lowered the kettlebell and let his arm hang limply.

"Do you know her?" I asked..

His grip tightened on the kettlebell's handlebar. "Did that psycho kill my Christa?"

My pulse picked up the pace. Erratic beats thumped against my ribcage. I'd struck gold.

"I–I don't think so," I said, the words tumbling over one another. It took all of my restraint not to demand he spill everything he knew about Blair. "The medical examination determined Christa's murderer was male. But I believe Blair was involved."

She was there, at least. A witness. A kidnapper. A cannibal.

I buried the latter thought. I'd reach Kai and Gerda before the witch hurt them—or Detective Wilhelm. There was no other option.

Alistair cursed again and called Blair a choice name relating to female dogs. "I knew it. Blair met Christa at a bar and it was around that same time Christa started acting crazy."

"Crazy?"

"I don't know," he said with a sigh. He bent to place the weight at his feet and then raked both hands through his thick blonde mane. His biceps bulged each time he threaded his fingers through his hair. "She was just cold and cruel. She'd randomly try to test my loyalty with weird riddles and she always wanted to be outside." He laughed without joy. "Even during a freaking snowstorm! I mean, she was always a little harsh, but I liked her that way. Then Blair came along and I barely saw Christa."

That certainly matched the Snow Queen's personality. "I need all the information you have on Blair."

"Will she get arrested?" he asked, suddenly wary. His eyes narrowed.

"As an accomplice to murder? Probably. Can you tell me more about her?"

Alistair shook his head. He nearly tripped on the kettlebell as he slowly backed away from the threshold. "No." With his eyes wide and jaw slack, it appeared fear had taken hold of him.

Then why the refusal to help? Hadn't he just described Blair as dangerous? The sudden switch didn't add up. Why protect the woman who'd possibly gotten his girlfriend into fatal trouble?

He hoisted the weight from the doorway and started to close the door in my face. My hand shot out and slammed against the door.

"Wait!"

"I can't help you," he growled. Fear quickly switched to anger. Fire flared in his gaze as he glared at me. The muscles in his forearms and biceps tensed as both of his hands curled into fists.

"You're looking really suspicious right now, Alistair," I said. It was low to stoop to threats, but I needed the information he had. Pregnancy strength had nothing on the massive, muscular man. He easily shoved the door shut, unencumbered by the pressure I put into keeping it open.

I banged my fist against the door and raised my voice. "Do you want the cops to come snooping around again? Should I tell them you have to exercise to keep yourself in check? What does that mean, Alistair? Are you dangerous?"

I pounded until my pinky finger, and the heel of my palm hurt. No sound came from the other side. What had triggered such a drastic change in his behavior? Did I first have to identify his fairy tale character and then use his story's plot to get to Blair? By the time I jumped through that many hoops, I'd have peed my pants. And Kai would be…*dead.*

I shook my head, refusing to believe it. I still had all night, until sunrise, to come up with a plan to keep power out of Wilhelm's hands and my husband alive.

"Alistair, open up," I begged. Excitement for answers shifted to immediate disappointment. My heart seemed to settle at the bottom of my stomach where Jack's weight pressed against my pelvic bone.

Please, help me. My fingers uncurled from a fist and my palm lay flat against the door. Jack sensed my stress and frost spread over my belly.

"Go away before I call security!" Alistair shouted.

What could I say that might convince him to share what he knew? *Nothing.* I knew nothing about the man. Threats didn't work. Something scared him more than the police discovering whatever he'd wanted to hide. His fear then manifested as an unhinged temper.

"Don't you want justice for Christa?" I asked.

A crash came from the other side. I guessed a barbell with weights heavier than I could even imagine had dropped to the floor. Stomping footsteps approached. Instead of opening the door, something slammed against it, likely his fist.

I stepped back, my chest heaving.

"Christa's dead," he said. "Leave, now."

My grip on the book tightened until my knuckles turned white. I lifted the book and stared at the title until desperation convinced me to spill the magic beans.

"This will sound crazy," I said. "But I need you hear me out. I believe Blair Danes is a witch. With magic, and everything."

Nothing happened. I hung my head and brushed my thumb over the embossed title. *Little Brother and Little Sister*. *Where is the witch keeping you, Kai?*

The quiet crick of an unhooked lock made my heart leap. The doorknob twisted, and the door creaked as Alistair cracked it.

"What did you say?" his voice was low, more of a grunt that words. But I understood him well enough.

I held up the book. "Blair is basically—well, no—she is the witch from this story. Whether or not you believe that, it doesn't matter. But you should know, I think Blair witnessed Christa's death. I don't know how she was involved, but she was there. If you help me find her, I can stop her from hurting anyone else. Like I said, I know it sounds nuts, but it felt right to be honest."

Alistair's Adam's apple bobbed as he swallowed hard. After a few moments of me staring at him, and him staring at the book, he opened the door wider.

"Come in," he said. His hand fell from the doorknob and his arms hung at his sides. He turned and walked away from the door. "You don't sound crazy." Though he was looking at the books on the shelf opposite the door, I knew he was addressing me.

I stepped across the threshold and followed him inside the humid room.

"Or maybe you do." He raised his hands behind his head and linked his fingers for a moment before dropping them. With a sigh, he turned to face me. "Maybe we've both lost our minds."

Alistair believed what I'd said. Somehow, he knew witches from fairy tales roamed San Francisco. Of course, only villains had ever known about the story aura when it had descended upon them. Did his self-awareness make him a dangerous antagonist?

I tensed at my stupidity. I'd entered his house, alone, without a clue to which story he belonged or if he'd become a villain.

"You wanted information on Blair, right?" he asked.

I nodded. "Right. Yes, I do." I cleared my throat and eyed him as he crossed the library to the home gym on the other side of the room.

All manner of exercise equipment from a weight rack to a treadmill filled the open space. I nearly choked on the thick air. Warmth didn't sit well with me anymore, not since I'd become pregnant with the essence of winter.

Alistair stooped to pick up a cell phone from a workout bench. The screen lit up from his touch. He tapped a few times before holding it out to show me a map.

"Take it," he said.

I stepped forward and did as he suggested. The maps app had a pin dropped near my side of the city. Close to Pioneer Park and the morgue where Reese worked, was a crematorium. The pin's red dot marked the building where bodies go to be cremated.

Alistair grunted as he pulled a tight workout T-shirt over his head. "That's where Blair works. I picked up Christa from there once."

A frown tugged at my mouth, and my heart skipped a beat. It both disturbed and excited me. My suspicions were confirmed. Blair Danes matched the characteristics of the witch from Hansel and Gretel's story. Even her job stayed true to the fairy tale's plot. A crematorium represented the evil woman's oven where she tried to cook children.

Is that where she's hiding you, Kai? I stared at the pin. The red dot marked the spot my husband might be bound and gagged. Was Detective Wilhelm there, too? Hopefully not. I wanted access to Kai before running into him again.

"Does that help?" Alistair asked.

I looked up, my eyes struggled to adjust from the phone to where Alistair had moved. He stood in front of the door with his hand on the knob.

"Yes," I said. "A lot, actually. Thank you."

He twisted the knob. "I'd take you there but…" his voice trailed and he shook his head. "Anyway, good luck." With that, he yanked the door open and waited beside it.

I nodded my thanks and marched across the room. I placed his phone in his palm before exiting and then stepped through the doorway.

When I turned to ask about what he believed, he'd almost closed the door. Through the crack I caught his face. His angled jaw and chiseled features drooped, almost as if melting. But it was only sadness that contorted his face. Anintense sadness that I recognized because I, too, felt the pain of loss.

My heart broke for the man who'd found his girlfriend murdered only days before. His grief was palpable, existing in the humid air that surrounded him. When the door shut, the lock clicked on the other side.

I shared in that pain, but it wasn't too late for the person I loved—I hoped. I turned from Alistair's apartment and hurried to the street. If I walked at my fastest pace, I'd make it to the crematorium before dark. Too bad my fastest pace was long before I'd hit the two-year pregnancy mark.

Still, I tried my best, letting my lungs squeeze and legs burn as I marched block after block. Brunchers had long gone home, and those who enjoyed the night life replaced them. What little sun had slipped through the cold, white day gave its last dying embers. Bar's neon signs flicked on while banks and boutiques closed.

The temperature dropped to unnatural levels again—a sudden dip. Those who braved the unpredictable chill scurried into the warmth of late-evening restaurants. The thawing I'd witnessed earlier felt like a fever dream now as frost coated every surface.

I glanced at the clock above the bank's door as I passed. According to the ticking timepiece, the day was almost done, and it'd only get colder.

T-minus ten hours until sunrise.

Chapter Sixteen

"I only appear to be dead."

— Hans Christian Andersen

I lost over an hour to waddling. Pregnancy put too much pressure on my bladder. I hoped to find a restroom after I saved my husband from a cannibal. As I looked ahead, I focused on putting one foot in front of the other.

Snowflakes swirled around me. The wind couldn't decide which direction to blow. It played with my hair, tossing it into my face and then slicing through the fabric of my hoodie. I knew, based on the white puffs that escaped with each breath, that the air had returned to Arctic temperatures.

While Jack protected me from the cold, I swore I'd protect Kai from the witch. Not even the brewing snowstorm could stop me.

The skin on my inner thighs chafed, and my feet screamed. Despite the pain, I didn't slow down until I turned onto Main street. The slanted sidewalk felt like scaling a mountain. I climbed the hill, doing my best to ignore the squeezing pain in my stomach. The tightness that started in my womb and radiated into my back forced me to slow down.

I seethed and pushed through the discomfort. After several rounds of false labor and Braxton Hicks contractions during my first pregnancy, I knew this wasn't the real deal. So instead of heading to the hospital to give birth, I continued to the place where people go when they die.

I didn't know what to expect when I arrived at the crematorium. Like other businesses that kept regular hours, its door was locked, and the lights were turned off. Thankfully, I knew my side of the city better than I knew Cheesecake Factory's menu. Though I'd never paid close attention to the crematorium before, I knew the layout of the streets. The building backed up to an alley which meant it had a secondary entrance.

If Kai was inside, I'd find a way to get to him. Or at least he'd hear me when I inevitably resorted to banging and shouting.

The long stretch of concrete glistened in the dim light that glowed from the single window at the back of the building. Ice covered the walkway where the sun hadn't reached. A rush of biting air blew my hair from my face as I stepped into the alley. At any other time, without Jack's magic, the chill would numb my nose and burn my lungs.

I hurried to the window. Through the curtain, I spied the movement of shadows. My heart flip-flopped with the excitement of confirmation. To assess the situation, I pressed my ear to the door. Only the sound of footsteps and a woman's mumbled voice broke the silence. I didn't give up hope. If the voice belonged to Blair Danes, I'd find Kai through her.

Snow streamed heavily now. White flecks blanketed my stomach's bump and snowflakes clung to my hair and eyelashes.

Despite the weather's warning to get inside, I hesitated. Unfortunately, I didn't have my gun, or anything else to defend myself with if she got violent. I'd need to play it cool through conversation.

"We're all about cool, right Jack?" I glanced at my stomach. Another rippling squeeze forced me to hold my breath. I exhaled and relaxed again. "I'll take that as a reminder that we're running out of time."

I knocked on the door. The woman's mumbles ended abruptly. Footsteps grew louder and the curtain in the window flickered, letting light flood the alley for half of a second. All fell silent again.

Thick snowfall deadened the sounds of the street. I no longer heard the roar of engines or booming music from passing cars.

After another knock, I caught the woman's curse. Muffled stomping came from the other side until the latch clicked.

Snowflakes spun around as the door swung open.

A young woman stood on the other side. She glared at me with bugged, emerald eyes and pinched lips. Her hair was dyed so platinum blonde it almost matched the snow and looked as fluffy. I guessed the shoulder-length hair had taken years of abuse from coloring chemicals and heated tools. Based on the silk white robe she had wrapped around her body, this woman had made the crematorium a home.

If I hadn't seen ghosts before—or rather, gods manifested as ghosts —I'd think this woman was haunting the building.

"Where's my order?" she asked. She tossed a book on a small table beside the door. I caught the title before it disappeared from my view. *The Lizzie Borden Murders Uncovered.*

I opened my mouth to respond, but the book caught me off guard. *Isn't that the lady who killed people with an ax?* A shudder rippled through me as my gaze met the woman on the other side of the threshold.

She fingered the tips of her fried hair. "Hello? Are you here to deliver my pizza or stare at me like an idiot?"

"Are you—" I cleared my threat and paused. For a moment, I let my investigator's brain take over. I scanned the scene for anything unusual, any clues. The back door appeared to open into a storage room. Pizza boxes, books, and papers buried a desk in the corner next to another door. Shelves filled with urns of all shapes and sizes lined the walls. Most of the urns were neutral colors from cream, to beige and ivory. The surroundings nearly camouflaged the woman in white.

"Yo, I'm freezing my butt off with this door open," she snapped. "Where is my freaking pizza?"

I glanced at the boxes on the desk and caught sight of a bit of snowflakes not yet melted on the top box. How many pizzas had this girl ordered in one night? Was she feeding two kidnapped adults?

No, it's her. It's the insatiable cravings, like Scarlet. I suspected only the fairy tale's food could satisfy her. And in Blair's case, that meant human flesh. I swallowed a gag. The tightening in my stomach didn't help with the queasiness that threatened to upend bile. I'd put nothing in my stomach since the plain oatmeal the police station fed those in the holding cell.

Blair suddenly lunged forward. In a protective reaction, I covered my stomach with my hands and dodged out of her way.

She raked her crazed gaze over me with her lip curled in disgust. Her neck stretched as she scanned the alley.

She cursed and repeated her question. "Where is my pepperoni and sausage? I'm ravenous!"

With the witch out of the way, a bright color among the muted shades caught my eye. Partially obscured by the desk, was the toe of a shiny, red rubber boot. Such a bold shade clearly didn't belong in the room or to the woman in white. It belonged to Gerda.

My heart beat faster and I stepped forward. Before I even realized what I was doing, I was inside, marching toward the desk. Crumpled on the other side, beside the rubber boots, was my sister-in-law's yellow raincoat.

"Hey! What the hell?" Blair shouted.

"They're here," I whispered. For a moment, I couldn't tear my eyes away from the shiny silver object nearly buried in the wrinkles of Gerda's raincoat. Dread filled me with a bitter sickness that sloshed at the pit of my stomach.

Kai's pocket watch locket. I grunted as I dipped to swipe the pocket watch from the pile. If the witch had removed their clothing and jewelry, did that mean I was too late?

"Are you some kind of thief? That's my stuff!" Blair stormed at me, hands on her hips.

Pumping adrenaline muted my nausea and boosted my energy. I straightened, shuffled to the other side of the desk, and headed for the other door. All thoughts of self-defensive reason slipped away and desperation clouded me. I wanted to find my husband and his sister. Now.

"Gerda!" I screamed. I scrambled for the door handle before Blair reached me.

Icy fingers dug into my forearm as she gripped me. I tried to yank away, but she had a firm grip. Sharp fingernails nearly pierced through my flesh and I yelped.

Jack reacted to the attack on his mother. Flesh turned to frost and frost turned to ice. My eyes widened at the sight of crackling ice crawling over Blair's bony fingers and thin wrist.

She gasped and wrenched her arm away, clutching it in her other hand. Icicles stretched and hung from her forearm as if on a house's gutters in the dead of winter. Even paler now, she'd become a ghost half wrapped in frost. The icicles already started to melt. Slow drips dropped from the sharp ends, staining the beige, spongy carpet.

To my advantage, it seemed she didn't notice the melting. Her jaw hung open as her eyes fixed on the pointed shards of ice that seemed to have grown from her wrist bone to her elbow.

"I can't feel my hand," she shrieked. Her voice was the equivalent of fingernails scraping against a chalkboard. "I can't move my fingers!"

Before the ice melted, I used my moment of opportunity and shoved through the door. The crematorium opened into a calming room with cushioned chairs and lamps holding warm yellow bulbs. Golden-framed pastoral paintings decorated the walls, making the room appear larger than it was with the faux glimpse of outside greenery. The room designed to comfort did nothing for my nerves.

"Kai! Gerda!" I shouted as I stumbled along.

Banging echoed from the other side of the building like fists pounding against a wall. I spun around and waddled toward the sound. Through a narrow hallway, I had to pass the storage room again. I moved as quickly as possible to avoid Blair's attention.

"I'm melting," she squealed. Out of the corner of my eye, I saw Blair on her knees still clutching her frozen hand. At any other time I'd smirk at the irony of the witch's words but Gerda's screams kept me pushing forward.

My palm pressed against the hallway's wall as I jogged. The crunch of the pocket watch's chain in my fist reminded me to hold on tightly. I closed my fingers around the gift Kai had considered his most precious belonging and used my wrist to support the bottom of my stomach. Through the pulsing adrenaline, I registered another contraction.

Not yet, Jack.

"Help!" A scream called out to me.

Where was my husband's voice? Adrenaline and fear combined to create the illusion of slowed time. The dim hallway elongated as if I ran through a fair's spooky funhouse rather than the city's crematorium.

"Help me!" Gerda slammed against the wall again.

I rounded the corner and spotted a door.

"I'm here," I said as my hand closed around the handle. When I jiggled it, the door wouldn't budge. I did my best to kick at the door but the weight of my stomach wouldn't let me lift my leg high enough. If I'd had my gun, I'd try shooting the locked handle, but I was empty-handed.

I uncurled my wrist to find the pocket watch.

"Mari?" Gerda said. "Is that you?"

"It's me, Gerda."

"You psycho!" Blair screamed.

I twisted my head and spotted the woman in white at the end of the shadowy hall. She charged at me, her hand dripping melted frost along the way.

The sight of snow gave me an idea. I wrapped my fingers around the handle and closed my eyes.

I miss you, Kai. I'm here to save you. I'm hurt without you. The last thought flooded my body with the ache of grief and Jack responded to my pain. Ice spread from my hand to the doorknob and the bolt inside the wall. The cold expanded the metal until it cracked.

The lock was weak enough for me to push through just in time. Blair's chilly fingertips brushed the back of my neck. Before her hands closed around my throat, I shoved into the locked room.

I fell into Gerda's arm. She stumbled back from the shock of it but quickly helped me straighten.

The room unsettled me. Two large cremation chambers inside of a brick wall were on the opposite side of the door. They reminded me of ovens. The feel of the room caused goosebumps to rise on my arms and neck.

Before the creepiness could sink too deep, Blair's attack threw my attention from the cannibal's story to immediate survival. I snapped my neck in the door's direction. The witch lunged at us, crazy eyes and all.

Just like her brother, Gerda packed a mean punch. Despite never having resorted violence in her life—until her life depended on it. Her fist connected with Blair's mouth and the witch's head knocked against the door frame. Of course, she didn't stay dazed for long. Not with the strength of the story aura that attempted to carry her through to the end. But in this fairy tale's plot, the story required both Hansel and Gretel to trick the witch before it'd end. I suspected Gerda wouldn't be able to seal the story on her own, which meant Blair would live on. For now. Where was Gretel's other half?

"Kai?" I breathed. I averted my eyes from the cremation chambers.

No. Don't think it.

I squeezed his pocket watch until my hand shook.

Blair shoved Gerda, and they engaged in an equal fight. Storybook character met storybook character with matched strength and speed. According to their tale, neither was meant to brawl and likely neither would find success. They were built—no written—for tricks.

I needed to join, to help Gerda bring Blair down so we could escape. But all the adrenaline coursing through my veins had frozen. I wondered if my blood could turn to literal ice from Jack's connection to me through the placenta. I breathe, much less move.

"Kai…" I repeated. It was all I could think, do, and say. Tears stung my eyes, and I squeezed them shut before I dared look at the cremation chambers again. Pain flared inside of me like an ice burn from within.

Blair huffed, trying to push Gerda off her feet. "Why did I listen to that bastard? I should have killed you so I didn't have to stay hungry."

The witch's words sickened me but I didn't have time to dwell on the icky feeling.

Where are you, Kai?

My womb contracted, tighter and longer now, sucking the breath from my lungs. I gripped the pocket watch tighter and tighter. When the contraction finally released, every emotion blasted me all at once and I screamed. Whether it was Kai's name or a cry of pain—more emotional than physical, even I didn't know.

Frost instantly covered me. When it spread from my feet to the floor, the walls, everywhere, it turned to ice. Though it only lasted a moment, a flash of a frozen domain within one second, it was long enough to win the fight.

Blair slipped on the slick surface and slammed her head against the ice. Gerda went with her but broke her fall on the witch's body. While Blair lay limp and unconscious, Gerda scrambled to her feet.

The ice had rescinded, disappearing as fast as it came and Gerda easily found her balance.

Without another thought, or another glance at the giant ovens, Gerda grabbed my arm and led me down the hall. We escaped through the storage room, not even stopping for her boots and coat.

The snowfall raged now. We stumbled out into the swirling white storm, blinded by winter. All at once, the adrenaline left me, my son's physical body manifested, and my legs shook. Unable to carry the weight of both Jack and the loss of my husband, I fell to my knees.

Packed snow crunched beneath my legs, and my hands disappeared into the white. I felt nothing. Even without Jack Frost's magic, the cold wouldn't bother me because I'd become wholly and entirely numb.

Chapter Seventeen

"Cowards die many times before their deaths; the valiant never taste of death but once."

— William Shakespeare

A disembodied voice called my name and pulled me from my daze. Tears blurred my vision. I blinked and made out the shape of a hand reaching through the white. Another contraction stiffened my stomach and sucked the breath from me.

"Mari?" Gerda repeated. Her palm turned up in an offer to help me to my feet. "Kai escaped."

I gasped for air, inhaling so desperately that my throat felt scratchy. Relief washed over me and the touch of the storm's panic registered across my skin again. I felt the wet snow on my legs, the fierce wind against my face, and Gerda's hand land on my shoulder.

"He's alive?" My voice cracked.

The wind whipped and carried it away but Gerda stepped close enough for me to see her. She nodded, understanding my outburst.

"I think so," she said. "When he woke up from whatever the witness drugged us with, he was stronger than her. He overpowered her and ran. He said he'd come back for me…" her words trailed and her brow furrowed. Gerda didn't look like herself without her glossy lip balm and bright shades of eyeshadow.

I accepted her hand. Thanks to her storybook strength, we didn't waste too much time getting me to my feet.

"What is it?" I asked.

"It was like he was two different people," she said. "One minute he wanted to help me and we schemed together like mischievous kids. Then the next he'd yell at me and say I was irritating him."

The troll mirror. Gerda had no idea the complexities of Kai's two tangled fates, neither of which he had control over. I knew why the story aura had chosen him to become the boy Kai. He was an innocent man in a big city who loved others dearly. Unfortunately, his character's adventure was to suffer the effects of the troll mirror when the shards of glass got into his eyes. The mirror made him see everything as ugly and bad.

But why is he Hansel, too? I racked my brain for Hansel's characteristics. The traits I could recall mirrored those of the boy Kai—sensitive, and a pure, innocent love for others. Was it more about the story than the character that had caused *Little Brother and Little Sister*'s story aura to connect with Kai?

"Do you know where he went?" I asked.

Gerda shook her head. "We need to leave," she said with a glance behind us.

Together, we limped from the alley. Snow swirled around us and the wind tried to knock us off our feet. Gerda's teeth chattered, and she shivered, clinging to my arm like life support. I didn't know if I felt warm to others, or cold, but I remained immune to the harsh weather.

Despite the rough conditions, I continued asking about Kai. How long ago had he escaped? Did he leave any hints about where he'd gone? Did Gerda see Detective Wilhelm at the crematorium? I filed away each answer as a clue and assigned each one a color in my mind's eye.

I pictured the timeline in orange. *Kai escaped this morning.* If he was out in this storm wearing nothing but the clothes he'd left with on the day of Christa's death, he might meet his own death from hypothermia.

According to Gerda, he'd said he was going to the story. I pictured the thought in yellow. What did that mean? Did he plan to go to the library? If he wanted to seal *Little Brother and Little Sister* he'd have stayed with Gerda and completed the plot at the crematorium. Or was his boy Kai personality more powerful at the moment he'd said it? Did that send him to Christa's body at the morgue to finish *The Snow Queen*?

In order to seal Andersen's tale, the character of Gerda would need to locate Kai. Of course, it was love that healed him from the shards of mirror glass and the real Gerda had little love for her brother. Did it matter since Christa was dead? We'd never seal that story.

Finally, in red, I noted the most important confirmation. *Detective Wilhelm was at the crematorium.* He was working with the witch, which meant he hadn't bluffed when he claimed to have Kai.

My muscle memory got us from the area near Pioneer Park to the staircase at my condominium building. I gripped the cold, metal banister and dragged myself up the stone steps. Gerda did the same, releasing her hold on me as the dangerous weather motivated her to climb quicker.

I rubbed the pocket watch's smooth surface with the thumb of my free hand. Despite my need to find Kai, and the clock's constant ticking, the storm forced me home.

Here, I'd leave Gerda in safety, grab my gun, and return to the streets. Somehow, someway, I had to find my husband before Detective Wilhelm got to him again.

By the time we made it inside, Gerda needed medical attention. She collapsed in a heap on the chair beside the couch. Scarlet scrambled to help while Wendy threw herself at me.

My daughter's little arms tried to wrap around my giant middle. Though it was late, hours past her bedtime, I didn't ask why she was still awake. Wendy missed her daddy as much as I did. Not only had he been missing from our lives for several days, but I was gone tonight too. The darkness of midnight during a snowstorm would have scared any kid. For a child who saw fairy tale monsters when she looked at men, Wendy braved the night.

I returned the hug with all the energy I had left. Before my belly crushed her slight frame, I released her and cupped her chin.

Enormous eyes stared up at me. Dark rings of exhaustion lined the skin under her lower eyelashes and worry creased her brow.

"Daddy's lost, isn't he?" she asked.

I opened my mouth but a painful lump in my throat made it impossible for me to admit the truth. I nodded. She deserved honesty.

"But I'm going to find him," I said. I tore my eyes from Wendy's gaze.

She nodded. "That's good. I think Uncle Carlos will need Daddy's advice on being a daddy."

I bit my lip and glanced at Scarlet who knelt in front of Gerda with a mixing bowl full of water. After she motioned for Gerda to sit forward, she gently pulled Gerda's hands over the bowl and submerged the frostbitten fingers into the water.

Finally, she met my gaze with a twinkle in her eye that confirmed the reason for her joy, her emotional turmoil, and her cravings. Scarlet was pregnant with Rapunzel. I wanted to pull her into a hug with tears of congratulations but we had more pressing matters to deal with.

To Gerda she said, "sit tight while I get you dry clothes." When Scarlet stood, she pointed to my soggy pants. "You too." She turned and jogged toward the bedroom.

"No," I said.

Scarlet paused in the doorway and raised her eyebrows.

"I'm going back out, to find Kai. He's alive somewhere and I have to get to him before Detective Wilhelm does."

She nodded. "Dry clothes then, at least."

"I'm fi—" Another contraction interrupted me. I cringed at the tightness in my stomach and the rippling ache over my tailbone. When it released, I repeated myself. "I'm fine."

Leave it to the former Keeper of Stories to understand. Nothing was going to stop me now. Not a storm. Not pain. Not even labor. Scar lifted her chin in a curt nod.

She passed through the kitchen, crossed the length of the living room, and then stopped in front of me. "Take your phone," she said as she grabbed my hand and pressed something into it. "Esmeralda stopped by and dropped it off along with the rest of the belongings left at the police station. She mentioned Wilhelm, too. I guess the whole precinct is worried about him. He hasn't shown up for work and was breaking a bunch of policies before."

"Sounds about right," I said. At least that proof would help me get him arrested later on. If I figured a way to get out of his trap.

"Promise to call me for help," she said, squeezing my hand.

I closed my fingers around the phone and then tucked it into my pocket. "I promise."

"Don't kill yourself," she said.

"I promise."

"To kill yourself?" she asked. She raised her eyebrow and gave me a skeptically smug look.

I rolled my eyes. "You know what I meant."

Scarlet accepted my answer and shifted her focus back to Gerda's first aid. After another hug from Wendy, I hurried into the back of the condo where I kept a safe hidden high in our bedroom closet. I clipped a holster onto my pants and secured my gun inside. When I emerged, I stayed out of the way, letting Scar and Wendy take care of my sister-in-law.

I quietly made my way to the door and slipped out with no more fuss.

Outside the wind howled its way through the open hall. I walked into it, bracing against the pressure of the storm's power. Hopefully, more walking wouldn't trigger the contractions to speed up.

I pulled my phone from my pocket and tapped the screen. It lit up with the picture that'd brought me to tears the day Kai went missing. What if Kai had escaped only to find himself in the clutches of detective Wilhem's killer hands? Why did Blair have Kai locked away if it was the detective who'd claimed to have him? The witch had mentioned listening to someone else, which kept Kai and Gerda alive.

Had they been working together? Did that make Wilhelm a character in Hansel and Gretel's tale?

I didn't think so. The only notable characters not already claimed were the children's father and stepmother. Though the stepmother was cruel and the father had abandoned them, neither matched Detective Wilhelm's desire for power. I'd yet to identify him, and if I found Kai first, I wouldn't need to.

I stared at my phone until the light blinked off. The clock had read twenty minutes after midnight.

T-Minus six hours until I'd meet a villain at the rift—the gateway to Storyland and living cut between worlds where power, magic, and immortality would be at the reach of my fingertips. And within Detective Wilhelm's grasp.

Chapter Eighteen

"The devil can cite Scripture for his purpose."

— William Shakespeare

Hunting a husband wasn't a far cry from hunting fairy tale villains. We'd fought on and off a lot lately, so I expected a struggle once I found him. Though it wouldn't be a battle like fighting the wolf or Dracula, I suspected he'd argue with me. If the story aura had convinced Kai to follow the Snow Queen, only love could save him. At least, that was how Hans Christian Andersen had written it.

But I wasn't the girl from the tale who saved the boy—Gerda was, or so I'd suspected. Wendy had never confirmed whether her aunt looked like the drawing of the girl in *The Snow Queen*. She'd only called her Gretel. So who was the girl from the tale? Without her, did I have any chance to find Kai?

I sank to the steps in front of the library. The storm raged around me, crystalizing ice on my eyelashes. A layer of snowflakes clung to my hair and clothes. If anybody else was stupid enough to brave the blizzard, they'd see a pregnant snow beast slumped on the sidewalk.

I dropped my head into my hands and let my heart sink to the pit of my stomach. I'd visited every location I suspected Kai would go. At the morgue, Eternity Eatery, and all of our favorites spots, I found nothing. No husband. No clues.

The phone in my lap lit up. It buzzed with Detective Wilhelm's name above a single text message.

Thirty minutes until sunrise.

I'd show up empty-handed. Had Detective Wilhelm found him? Did that make him the character of Gerda from *The Snow Queen*? Impossible. Gerda was kind and loved her friend dearly.

I tapped a response. *You're bluffing. You don't have Kai.*

Three dots popped up, and I waited, not breathing, until the message delivered.

Are you willing to risk that?

I wanted to throw my phone across the street. My fingers closed tightly around it as another contraction rippled through me. They came faster now with twice the force like a vice gripping my womb. Jagged pain radiated up my back. The ache forced me to lean forward and take a moment for slow breaths.

When the contraction subsided, I registered a faint vibration in my hand. Another message from Detective Wilhelm lit up the screen.

That's what I thought.

"Screw you," I cursed.

I dragged myself to my feet and started the trek to Pioneer Park. Without Jack's magic keeping me warm in the snow, I'd be dead by now. Instead, my feet moved forward, and I clung to the hope that the detective no longer had leverage.

Every few steps, labor forced me to stop. I'd pause, right there in the middle of the sidewalk, and double over. In quiet pain, I waited for the contraction to finish and then I straightened and pushed through the wind. Thankfully, the storm eased slightly, and the wind didn't whip with as much force as it had earlier.

The blinding white storm slowly faded. My surroundings were visible now, though coated in a thick layer of snow. A shiver stole down my spine and the chill of the weather gradually seemed to seep into me.

After another contraction, goosebumps covered my arms and neck. The hoodie was no longer enough to keep me from shaking. I tugged the hood over my head and bristled at the thought of Red Riding's hood—the object that'd dragged me into this life.

In moments, I'd see it again, peeling away from the rift between worlds.

Too many memories flooded me when I stepped into Pioneer Park. The sight of the bench sent me back to our early marriage when I'd shared takeout meals with my husband after long days at work. On the play structure, I recalled Wendy playing with the boy who'd become Tinker Bell. I squinted at the pathways that led deeper through the trees. There, I'd witnessed the wolf transform for the first time, long before I knew stories were real.

At one time, in a dream, I saw Shere Khan perched in the trees that created shadows across the park. I stopped and reached for a lamppost to steady myself. Labor steadily grew more powerful while the storm did the opposite.

A humming laugh caught my attention. I looked up from my stomach. Detective Wilhelm stood by the diamond in the rift. His feet were splayed wide, a hint at his arrogance. He kept his hands tucked into his coat pockets and his chin tilted down. Through thick eyebrows, he glared at me with a smirk curling his mouth.

He was the picture of villainy, though he wielded no weapon or magic. Yet.

I frantically scanned the park for Kai. Snow fell steadily but gently—not thick enough to block the view of another person. Still, I spied no sight of my husband.

"A bluff," I breathed.

In a moment, I expected Detective Wilhelm to reveal a gun from beneath his coat. He'd aim it between my eyes, or perhaps at my stomach, and hold another loved one hostage at the end of the barrel. I had my weapon holstered and concealed to fight back, but the pain of labor made me sluggish. Maybe we'd get caught in a duel, like two cowboys from the old West. Or maybe, I'd walked into a trap I couldn't yet see.

Detective Wilhelm shook his head.

I straightened and waddled closer. If anything, closing the distance between us would help me aim easier.

"You lied," I said. "Kai got away from you, didn't he?"

He sniffed and wiped at his leaky nose. "I don't need him."

"But you said—"

"I don't have to touch a hair on his head," he interrupted. "Your husband will kill himself."

"Where is he?"

Detective Wilhelm pulled his hands from his pocket and pinched the stretched square of fabric. The red flap looked like blood in the cut between worlds. But it'd never scab, never heal, unless I found away to close the rift again.

"I'll tell you, if you if you remove this," he said.

A slick wetness covered my body as my clothes clung to my skin. I only just noticed, or Jack's magic was slipping.

"What's stopping me from walking away and searching on my own?" I asked.

He sighed and held out his hand. In moments, the snow covered his palm. "Do you see this? People can't survive cold for too long. But you can get to him in time, if you do what I've asked." He shook off the snow and grabbed the flap of fabric again.

"Why do you want the hood?" I asked. "It's bound to me. You won't get its magic." It was my turn to bluff. Though the hood behaved that way in the past, everything had changed when I'd sacrificed it to stop the magic that flowed from Storyland. If the way the story aura interacted with our world had been altered, the hood probably was too.

He shook his head. "I don't want it. I want you to wear it."

My stomach turned sour. What could he possibly want with that? Was this some sick fantasy of the man I'd worked alongside for so many years?

He took a step closer and stared down his nose at me. Had he grown taller? Or was it the story aura that made him appear larger and more menacing? Would I ever know which tale had chosen him?

"I want my immortality back," he said.

"It won't last," I said. "The story protection only works until the plot ends." *Ebenezer Scrooge. Why'd I say that?* Equipping the villain with extra knowledge wouldn't do me any favors. I expected a demand to come next. He'd force me to promise not to touch his story's plot. That way he'd live forever in an unending existence as a villain.

"You don't know who I am. Do you?" A twinkle shined in his ugly eyes.

I scoffed. "Are you going to tell me you're my father?" Scarlet's movie references flashed in my mind. Leave it to me to joke at an inappropriate time. At least it eased my thumping heart.

He laughed again. The rough, sickening sound had me reaching for the holster at my side.

"I wouldn't do that if I were you," he said. "If you shoot me, you'll never find Kai in time. I give him about ten minutes before hypothermia kills him. He's a character, so he's strong, but it's been a long night. Ten minutes, Rowan."

The erratic tick of my pulse ramped my nerves. I curled and uncurled my fist. The cold bit into my bare fingers but I resisted putting my hands inside my pockets. Though it'd protect my skin from the frost, I'd be vulnerable if Wilhelm decided he'd lost his patience with me.

I spoke up. "Do you really want immortality when you'll spend an eternity in prison?"

His eyes narrowed, but he remained silent.

"Why did you kill Christa?" I didn't know why I asked. Why did I waste precious seconds when my husband was about to succumb to the elements? Maybe I hoped I was wrong. Maybe he'd say it was an accident.

"It was an accident," he said through his teeth.

Had I imagined that? *Dang, I'm good.* If I kept him talking, maybe I'd determine his identity. Maybe I'd make a bargain with him to let his story continue for a certain number of years. Maybe I'd stop this nonsense before I resorted to tearing the hood off the rift and let story after story spill into our world. Magic would run rampant—a changed magic that I didn't fully understand.

"The hood, Mari," he growled, his voice rough and low, exactly as Tala had described.

A gust of wind swept through the center of Pioneer Park. My whole body shook from the chill of the icy air.

"I don't understand," I said. "Were you working with the Snow Queen? Was it really an accident or will you kill the witch, too?"

"Wouldn't that help you and your lost husband?"

I shook my head. "Not if it won't seal his story."

Another laugh. Apparently, my understanding of Storyland's magic amused him.

"Explain the accident," I demanded. I'd have to dig through my mind to match his story with a fairy tale, but it was worth a shot.

He pinched the bridge of his nose and frowned. "Kai is going to die—"

"What did Christa ever do to you?" I asked. "Were you in some kind of evil villain team together? Did she want to turn good? She was a neutral antagonist, you know? So why choose her—"

"It was supposed to be you!" he shouted. Red flushed over his cheeks and neck and his mouth twitched as it held a grimace. Quickly, his anger faded and the hint of a smile flickered across his face. "But it's a good thing it wasn't. I didn't know only you could remove the hood. I thought you'd be wearing it. I thought I'd end you and take immortality for myself."

Bile burned in my throat. A contraction came at the worse time, stripping me of focus and suffocating my torso with the intensity of nearing labor. Physical pain spotted my vision, but it paled in comparison with the shock from his confession.

Fear struck as his gaze bore through me, hungry for my blood. Thankfully, not literally, like Hansel and Gretel's witch.

He shook his head. "She was supposed to lure you out into the storm through Kai's story. I knew you'd follow to save him. She planned a blizzard to disorient him. I'd place the weapon in his hands and he'd be arrested for the murder of his wife. Simple as that."

Sick. The twisted bastard deserved a bullet.

He swallowed hard, and his gaze dropped slightly. "But I acted too fast and I sometimes I can't remember what its like to be human. I didn't mean to hurt her. We belonged in the same…" his voice cracked.

That explained his odd behavior at the crime scene. Detective Wilhelm was mourning his mistake while simultaneously trying to determine how to pin the murder on me.

"Belonged to the same what? The same story as Christa?" As soon as I said it, I could have sworn a lightbulb appeared above my head the way portals appeared at Scarlet's whim when she was the Keeper of Stories.

Detective Wilhelm was from *The Snow Queen*.

He'd made a mistake. A mistake. Repeating the word helped pieces of the puzzle come together. The character who messed up the most in *The Snow Queen* was the unnamed one—the one I'd glossed over. I hadn't even considered him a character of the plot since he only appeared at the beginning to trigger the story of the troll mirror.

"You're the devil," I breathed. His behavior at the crime scene made sense. "You were concealing that side of you."

Detective Wilhelm blinked slowly, shifting his gaze to meet mine again. "It wasn't easy pretending to be human again."

As the devil, it made sense why he thought he'd remain immortal, even beyond the story's end. All he wanted was for me to take the hood.

Take the hood and Kai lives.

"How can I be sure Kai is still alive?" I asked.

He smiled. "I repeat, are you willing to take that risk?" With all the arrogance in the world, he stretched out his hand. He wasn't offering it to me, he was making a point. Despite the calmer storm, it was still snowing, still freezing.

I could shoot him, but how would I find Kai without his help?

My heart skipped a beat. The plot of *The Snow Queen* mostly consisted of the girl's search for her friend Kai. She loved him dearly and spent the entire story trying to find him. It was exactly what I'd done all night in the storm. She even made trades with the people she met along the way to help find her friend.

I'm the girl Gerda. I was the one who loved Kai dearly. *I* was the one willing to do anything to find him. Of course the story aura had chosen me.

Then why hadn't Wendy see the character within me? Was what I'd called pregnancy strength really my storybook power this whole time?

I placed my palm on my stomach. Jack's magic was more powerful than anything *The Snow Queen* girl had. He was stronger, even, than the queen. Christa had said so herself. Maybe Wendy couldn't see past what she'd called *Elsa* from Disney's version of *The Snow Queen*.

I lifted my chin, meeting Wilhelm's arrogance with confidence. "If I take the hood, we both become immortal at the same time." *Maybe.* "You won't be able to kill me and I won't be able to kill you." *Maybe.* I sucked in a breath. The chilled air hurt my lungs, burning like ice against bare skin. "But I'm mortal now, and I'm willing to bet you have a gun on you."

I reached for my weapon. I raised it with my palms turned out and slowly surrendered it to the snow on the ground. His narrowed eyes followed my every move, curious and dark.

"If I don't take the hood, you can—" Another contraction interrupted me. If my crude calculations were right, the contractions came every six or seven minutes. I was officially in labor. Jack would be here soon and he'd be safe from Detective Wilhelm's weapon.

But I didn't need immortality to save me. I only needed to find Kai which would seal *The Snow Queen.* Detective Wilhelm would return to his status as a man without the storybook strength. He wouldn't need me to take the hood, because it couldn't make a non-character immortal.

I spoke again, "If I don't take the hood, you can shoot me."

"Why would I do that? I need you—"

"Because I'll take the hood to save my life," I lied. He believed he'd live on as the devil, but I knew he was merely a troll, a character created by Andersen named after a hellish demon. "Do you really think I'll let my newborn son go without meeting his mother?"

"Take it now and you won't have to make a deal with the devil." He nodded toward the flap of fabric.

"You said so yourself, Kai only has minutes left."

His jaw shifted back and forth as he gritted his teeth. I let him chew on the trade while I braced for another contraction.

"Please," I begged. "All I want is for you to take me to him. Then you can live forever and I'll never tell anyone that you killed Christa."

With that offer, he raised his eyebrows. I'd piqued his interest. His guilt over the accidental killing clearly haunted him. Or maybe it was embarrassment. Like the devil in Andersen's tale, he'd humiliated himself with a mistake. In the story, he dropped the mirror. In real life, he'd dropped a tire iron against his confidant's head. The humanity of feelings alone told me he was a person with a character's fate—not an immortal being from hell.

"After you take the hood, you'll solve the murder," he said. "You'll determine the killer Blair Danes and you'll tell the precinct that I'm in witness protection because she's after me."

"Fine," I agreed.

He nodded and thrust out his hand. When I took it, I nearly threw up on his arm. I hated to feel his hand in mine, to touch the hand that'd brutally beat a woman to death.

With the agreement completed, Detective Wilhelm turned and headed down a branched pathway through the woods of Pioneer Park. I followed in his wake.

I gasped as a contraction nearly crippled me. It forced me to stop and bend over. I reached for a lamppost that marked the entrance of the walkway to steady myself.

Detective Wilhelm snorted and tossed me a careless glance. "Don't worry, he's close."

When I looked up, I caught sight of his cruel grin before he turned away from me. If I didn't know he was a character, I'd hate myself for what I'd done. A sliver of that hate still stewed within me at the sight of his disturbing arrogance.

I'd just made a deal with the devil—as written by Hans Christian Andersen.

Chapter Nineteen

"The course of true love never did run smooth."

— William Shakespeare

Detective devil kept good on his promise. He led me down the pathway and stopped at a bridge that crossed over a small stream. When he pointed over the wooden railing at the water below, I saw it'd frozen from the supernatural storm. No longer did the stream trickle over smooth rocks and offer calming white noise for runners and dog walkers.

As if on cue, a contraction tightened my torso. Every muscle in my body tensed as I fought through the pain and scanned the ice below.

"There," Detective Wilhelm said. He used his gun to point to a lump in the snow then quickly aimed the barrel at me again.

My heart slammed into the depths of my stomach. A coating of snow camouflaged the shape of a body. Lean limbs were splayed limp over the ice. Tears and rage and adrenaline bubbled inside of me.

"Kai!" I sobbed.

I stepped off the wooden slats of the bridge and scrambled down the bank. Snow fell from bushes and branches as I shoved my way through, slogging over weeds. The mud on the bank had turned slick and solid in the freezing weather. My foot slid out from underneath me.

I leaned into the slip and let my knees hit the hard ice. Cracks rippled out from where I'd fallen, spreading and reaching all the way to the outline of my husband buried in the snow.

"Kai, can you hear me?" I crawled toward him and tucked my legs underneath me.

I was on my knees in front of my husband's body, begging for him to hang on with every beat of my heart.

He lay flat against the icy stream with his eyes closed. Frantically, and ignoring the bite of the snow on my fingers, I brushed the white off of his face. A thin layer of ice covered every surface of exposed skin. His shaggy, wet hair had turned solid. Frost collected on his eyebrows and eyelashes and his lips were blue.

"No." Tears spilled over my cheeks and sorrow seemed to congeal my blood. It felt like a dream where I couldn't move fast enough. My heart was too heavy to pump my blood and keep my limbs working. Grief held my entire body hostage as I succumbed to aches and sluggishness.

I pulled his head into my lap, and it lolled to the side. His limp neck failed to support the weight of it. Salt stung where my dry lips had cracked. Finally, violent, loud sobs overtook me and shook my shoulders as if possessed by a hellish heartbreak.

A contraction squeezed inside of me but I ignored the pain. Not even labor distracted me from the devastating sight.

"Kai…" The choking emotion in my throat cut off my voice. "Kai, please."

I cupped his face in one hand and felt for breath beneath his nose with the other. At his throat, I pressed two fingers and waited for the thud of his pulse, however faint.

I didn't breathe. I couldn't. Waiting for the confirmation of life from his stiff body sucked the last bit of hope from my spirit. As if Detective Wilhelm was truly the devil, it seemed he'd led me to the moment my soul departed my body.

"I don't believe it," I spoke between sobs. "You can't be gone."

I can't live without you.

I pulled Kai's heavy body closer to me into a desperate hug. Tears dripped from my chin and splashed against the hard surface of ice over his cheeks. I tucked my chin into my chest and pressed my forehead against his.

I whispered, "I love you."

I know, he'd say. But he didn't. His frozen lips would never move again.

Like a bolt shifting in a door's lock, something inside of me snapped. Rage shoved anguish aside. My cheek twitched where tears had dried and tightened the skin with salt. I blinked, rolling my eyes to stare at the man who stood above me.

Detective Wilhelm gazed down at me, void of emotion.

"We had a deal," I said. My voice was low and hoarse.

The hint of a brazen smile quivered over his lips. "I said I'd take you to him, not that he'd be alive. The best part is, I still get to shoot you." He folded his arms across his chest. "If you don't wear the hood."

This wasn't how the story ended. Sure, I'd twisted tales before, but Andersen's conclusion to this plot was one I intended to keep intact. In the original ending, Gerda found Kai, she saved his life, and then they returned home where summer began. The girl's warm tears and kisses saved him.

The Snow Queen wasn't over. I refused to accept 'the end'.

"I love you," I said again. "Love saves you. I know it does. It can't be too late."

A contraction left me breathless, and a cry escaped me before it released. The intense pain and pressure demanded my attention. I sucked in cold air and exhaled a puff of white.

"You can't leave me," I continued, holding Kai close to me—close to his son. "There's no way in wonderland I'm letting you get out of changing diapers that easily." An awkward laugh slipped out of me as tears welled in my eyes again. "You still have to put Jack's picture on the other side of my locket." When I reached for the necklace, I found nothing. It was still at home where officer Esmeralda had brought it from the police station.

Instead, I dug into my pocket and produced the pocket watch. With a flick of my thumb, I popped it open. The clock didn't matter to me now because time had already run out. My eyes trailed the rim of the silver frame that held our family picture. We'd planned to update it when our son arrived.

"My turn," Detective Wilhelm said. "You've had enough time."

I ignored him, refusing to give him the obedience he craved. He'd begged me to say he was right, to give him permission to control me, during the interrogation. Now, I wouldn't even look at him.

"I hate to say it," he said with a sniff. "Actually, I don't. This is a perfect example of why you must wear the hood. All the characters will be immortal again. If you'd just taken it when I said, maybe Kai would still be alive."

His words should have ignited my rage again, but I didn't have enough energy. Another contraction overwhelmed me. They came too fast now, threatening to push Jack from his home of two years. Cramping pain surged through my belly and back and the pocket watch almost slipped through my fingers.

When it passed, I opened my palm and stared at the item Kai had considered his most prized possession. The silver caught a gleam of sunlight. I looked up, squinting at the stream of yellow shining through the trees. It cast a bright glow across the frozen stream.

The storm had broken along with my heart.

I slipped my fingers into Kai's limp hand and let go of the pocket watch. When I pulled my hand away, a glimmer drew my eye. The carvings in the silver caught the shine of the sun. I'd forgotten I'd had the back of the pocket watch engraved. In sprawling, cursive letters it read *I'm lost without you.*

"That's why you're Hansel," I whispered. We'd both become lost with the distance between us. "But I couldn't be Gretel, since she's your sister." I laughed without joy.

"Rowan, I'm losing my patience," Detective Wilhelm said.

I didn't so much as glance at the man holding me at gunpoint but I registered his voice somewhere behind me. I couldn't tear my eyes from the locket's engraving.

The ice coating Kai's fingers grew soft and slid from his flesh.

My heart skipped a beat. Was it the trick of the sunlight or did his hand twitch?

The melting started at the center of his palm and slowly spread over his wrist and then crawled up his arm. Time stood still as the ice sloughed off his skin. I could have sworn the watch itself no longer ticked away the seconds, but froze as it, too, waited for its owner to move.

Kai curled his fingers around the pocket watch and the locket clicked shut.

My tears returned, slipping one by one down to my chin. They raced to drip onto my hoodie and Kai's shirt where the wetness left dark spots. Joy swelled in my heart and warmed me from the inside out.

He blinked slowly, and his lips parted where a swirl of white breath escaped. I cupped the back of his neck to help him lift his head.

"You're alive," I said.

His eyes shifted to meet mine, but he didn't hold my gaze for long. He flicked his attention to something above my head. The crunch of snow beneath boots came from behind me.

"Mari." Kai coughed.

It was a warning. Before I could react, the hard barrel of a gun pressed against my temple.

Chapter Twenty

"**Y**ou have a promise to keep," Detective Wilhelm said.

A deal with the devil. But he was no longer the character from *The Snow Queen*. None of us were bound by Hans Christian Andersen's plot any longer. But the detective didn't know that.

Only I knew Kai was still a storybook character while Wilhelm and I had both lost our extra strength and speed.

The squeeze of the most intense contraction forced a whimper from me. Kai's brow twisted in concern.

"You're in labor," he said.

"And you're dead if your wife doesn't get moving," Detective Wilhelm said. He used the weapon to wave Kai to stand.

Slowly, Kai rolled to his side, ice sloughing off of him with every move. Despite having just been frozen, he didn't so much as flinch as he pulled his legs under him. He slipped the pocket watch into the pocket of his pants and straightened. On his knees now, he reached out and tucked my tangled hair behind my ear. Only moments ago, he'd succumbed to frost, and now, his eyes were bright with the life of an energetic boy. As Hansel, Kai carried the fiery determination of a young man willing to risk it all to save another's life.

I wasn't Gretel, but together, we'd take down the man holding us hostage. I hoped.

A lump gathered in my throat. It was a flimsy plan and labor might throw a wrench into it. Another contraction sent waves of pain that undulated through my back, belly, and hips.

"Mari needs to get to a hospital," Kai said, shooting the detective a glare.

"I'm okay," I breathed as the squeezing subsided. "I have you, and you're stronger than *anyone*." With the last word, I elongated the vowels and flicked my eyebrows. Though Kai didn't know about the character's extra strength and speed, I knew he trusted me. I rolled my eyes in the detective's direction and kept my head still. The gun's barrel felt cold and slick as Detective Wilhelm jammed it against my skull again.

"Now," Detective Wilhelm growled.

"I love you, because you're the strongest." I said, to drive the point home.

Kai shifted his gaze between us. "I know," he said.

Together, we climbed to our feet while the detective watched. Groans of impatience came from Wilhelm and I tensed, hoping he wouldn't lose it and put a bullet in us both.

I thought back to how the magic had changed. Even with the storybook strength and speed, Detective Wilhelm's unnatural swing against Christa's head hadn't killed her. Storybook characters were no longer immortal, but they were unnatural.

The thought sparked hope for us. I struggled up the slick bank, tripping over roots and branches along the way. The ripple of a fierce contraction caused my foot to slip.

Kai, forgetting about the gun hovering behind us, broke from his climb and grabbed my elbow. I gasped as he caught me, not out of shock or even pain, but the fear that his obvious speed had revealed itself to the detective.

"Hands off of her," Detective Wilhelm barked. He waved the gun to show that Kai needed to step away from me. "Show me your hands."

Kai did as he was told, revealing his empty palms in momentary surrender. While I faced away from Detective Wilhelm, I mouthed a message to Kai.

You're stronger. My lips formed around the words and recognition flickered in his eyes.

He turned, and we continued through the bushes, and weeds until we made it to the concrete sidewalk. With the bridge behind us, we headed for the glow of the lampposts that stood as pillars at the end of the walkway.

With each step, my heart thumped harder. Moments of opportunity slipped away the closer we came to the rift. I had no doubt that the detective would take me up on the offer to shoot me and force me to save my own life with the hood.

He was the lowest of low as villains go. Was *being the key word.*

I scraped a plan together. Once we reached the rift, the detective would surely point the weapon at me. Without the gun's barrel balanced between the two of us, it'd give Kai an opening. I glanced at Kai, hoping he'd notice my gaze on him.

The tree cover thinned as we reached the center of Pioneer Park. We emerged from the branching pathway into the open area of concrete with the play structure to our left and the diamond in the rift straight ahead.

Finally, Kai spied me watching him. With his attention, I gave a discreet nod toward the rift. Hopefully, it was enough.

Sunlight shone through the spared branches and cast twisting patterns of yellow on the wet ground. Wherever the sun reached, the snow had already melted.

I breathed through more rippling contractions. We were only steps away from the square of red fabric.

"Take the hood," Detective Wilhelm said as soon as we reached the rift.

The gun clicked, ready to shoot. My pulse pounded through my temples, shoving blood through my veins as fast as possible. Nerves left my fingers twitching as I felt for the soft velvet.

"I won't say it again," he said.

Kai stood at my side. It'd only take a flick of Wilhelm's wrist to aim at him instead of me. I turned and put both hands on the hood to show the detective I was committed to my promise.

I closed my fingers around the fabric that belonged to the bane of my existence. Still, I couldn't bring myself to remove it, to allow more villains to flood our world and trap me in an unending cycle of sealing stories.

Impatient, the detective brought his other arm up to support the weapon. With both hands on the gun, I knew he'd fire it any second.

In reaction, I tugged at the fabric. Easily, the tendrils of magic that'd sewn the hood and the rift together unraveled at my touch. Several inches pulled away, revealing Storyland's array of colors.

A blinding brightness caught my eye opposite the rift. A sheen of sweat beaded on Detective Wilhelm's forehead. The sunshine caught the shiny wetness of his brow and he squinted in the light.

"Now," I breathed.

My voice triggered a reaction from both the detective and my husband. The deafening roar of the gun stopped my heartbeat.

Kai barrelled into him faster than I could gasp.

In a moment, I expected to be crumpled over and bleeding on a shrinking patch of snow. If he was smart, the detective wouldn't shoot to kill, just aimed in a spot that'd force me to take the hood before I bled out.

Lightning agony tore through me, but I didn't fall. I didn't bleed. Instead, water spilled down my legs, soaking through my pants from the crotch down.

Before I could make sense of the situation, Kai scrambled to his feet. He gasped and choked for breath. I raked my eyes over his body but didn't spot any blood on him either.

Instead, dark red pooled out on the concrete in front of us. Detective Wilhelm's shiny head had hit a spot where the sun shone. The snow had already melted and his skull had cracked against the solid ground.

The gun had fallen from his limp fingers. His eyes stared up at nothing, unblinking and frozen in time.

"I killed him," Kai said through shaking breaths. He stumbled back and ran both hands through his hair as he nearly bumped into me. "I am a killer."

He shook his head, never breaking his gaze on the body before us. I cupped his bicep, both to steady myself as a stronger contraction shuddered through me and to comfort him.

"I didn't mean to," he said.

"It was self defense," I said.

"Blair told me I killed Christa, and I didn't want to believe it. But she insisted it was what she'd witnessed, and I felt so sick about it. And then I came out here, because I thought—" his voice cracked. He shook his head again. "I thought maybe if I finished the Snow Queen's story that she'd come back to life, somehow."

My heart ached for him and what he must have gone through over the past few days. While I had searched for him and had worried for his life, he'd suffered the guilt of murder and two controlling storylines pulling him across different plot threads.

"Kai, you saved my life."

At that, he whipped around. He ran his hands over my arms and scanned me. "You're okay. I tried to get to him before he shot—"

"Yes, I'm okay."

Tension in his shoulders dissipated, and his arms dropped. A second later, he pulled me into a hug. I couldn't return the display of affection. The contractions fought for my attention, coming ten times faster now.

I groaned from the crack of pain that radiated up my spine.

"Call Scarlet," I said as I slowly knelt to the ground. Kai supported my weight and crouched with me.

"Scarlet?" he asked.

I nodded, breathing through a contraction that screamed *its time to push*. "To get the cops. They'll know it was self-defense since he's been obsessive and skipping work and—Ebenezer Scrooge!" I screamed.

"What? What?" Kai grabbed my hand and squeezed. If he wasn't careful, he'd pop my fingers right off my hand. I knew he was worried that the bullet had hit me all over again.

"My phone…in my pocket," I squeaked. With shaking hands, I unbuttoned my pants. As unpleasant as it was to go pantsless in the middle of the park, I needed the space to give birth.

Kai nodded and let go of me. He dug for my phone in my pants where the band now cut into my thighs. Quickly, he tapped Scarlet's contact info on the screen.

My hands splayed on the concrete as I eased back and forth on my knees. Any second now, another contraction would demand I start pushing. Jack would be here, born in front of a dead body.

My stomach twisted at the thought. I wanted to stand, to call an ambulance, to cry for a cab to take me to the hospital or home. I opened my mouth, not sure of which to ask for, when a scream echoed behind me.

The pitch of the woman's voice exploded through my skull. I pushed back into a crouch and slapped my hand to my ears to block the piercing sound. My eyes scanned for the source of the scream but nobody had joined us in Pioneer Park.

All fell silent again, for a moment. The woman's voice cut through my groaning as labor demanded I focus on pushing a child's body out of my own.

"He's been shot!"

Chapter Twenty-One

"Now then, let us begin. When we are at the end of the story, we shall know more than we know now: but to begin."

— Hans Christian Andersen, *The Snow Queen*

To my absolute delight, the labor slowed enough for me to get away from a dead man. I gripped the side of the plastic slide where Wendy had played with her friend Tinker Bell. The only child on the playground today would be Jack.

The short walk from the rift to the play structure, gave me distance from the blood and the weapon that'd nearly ended my life. I'd begged Kai to help me sit down where I could lay back if needed. The slide was the best option, since the plastic was softer than the hard metal benches and the cold, concrete ground.

I screamed at the pressure inside of me. My lungs belted the sound that rivaled the unknown woman's cries. After only a few pushes, Jack was out. Wendy had wailed and cried when she came into the world, but Jack remained calm as he blinked silently at his father.

Kai held him in his bloody hands and arms. We'd delivered our son, alone, on the playground. Relief replaced adrenaline and my muscles melted into the plastic slide.

I breathed long enough to wonder about the source of the unidentified scream.

Sirens replaced my thoughts, and pressure rippled through me again. My body's insistence to finish labor demanded I focus on the situation at hand. I still needed to deliver the placenta.

Car brakes screeched on the road beyond the walkways. Red and blue lights flashed through the trees just outside the park. Thankfully, an ambulance arrived just after cops flooded the park, led by officer Esmeralda.

The rest of the morning was a blur. The emergency response team helped with the rest of Jack's birth, cutting the cord and cleaning him off. A man wrapped Jack in a paper-thin blanket, and it was only then I realized the weather had grown hot.

All the snow was gone, not even remnants of wetness remained. The sun beat down on the playground where it split through the trees. Sweat coated my brow, upper lip, and soaked my underarms. A blonde EMT helped me to my feet and guided me to the ambulance where she insisted on checking my blood pressure. There, she also verified the strength of Jack's pulse which resulted in wide eyes.

Likely, his heart beat faster than one she'd heard before, but I didn't let her overthink it. I insisted she hand him over so I could attempt to breastfeed. Knowing my last experience, it was the start of a failed effort. Still, I wanted to try.

After two years of cooking inside my womb, I expected my son to be bigger. Jack blinked up at me with crystal blue eyes. He was more alert than I'd ever witnessed a baby behave, and only minutes after birth, but he wasn't big.

"What does he weigh?" I asked.

"Five pounds, five ounces," the EMT said as she filled out paperwork on a clipboard. "And as healthy as a horse. But you lost a little more blood than you should have. We'll take you to the hospital to be watched for twenty-four hours."

I nodded. A comfortable, clean bed in a quiet space sounded like heaven.

Kai appeared at the back of the ambulance. He breathed heavily after having jogged out to the street.

"I need to stay and answer Esmeralda's questions," he said.

"Is everything okay?" I asked.

He nodded which knocked his messy hair into his eyes. With the swipe of his hand, he brushed it away. "She said everyone was worried about Detective Wilhelm's behavior. They know he was trying to frame us."

"How?" I tried to straighten as I adjusted the bundle of joy in my arms. Jack stayed calm, the perfect behavior I needed from him right now. Maybe he sensed my needs the way he had when he was growing inside of me.

"Reese is here, he said he has proof that Wilhelm killed Christa."

The shoes. Scarlet must have called him.

Jack squirmed in my arms, breaking a tiny fist through the loose swaddle. His mouth split open with a slow yawn. A smile tugged at my lips.

When I looked up again, Kai mirrored my faint expression of joy. After a torrential few days and a terrible storm, we were finally at peace.

"I love you," he said.

"I know."

The EMT pulled the doors shut, but I kept my eyes on the park as we drove away. Through the back window, I spied the walkway that led into Pioneer Park, the place where the diamond in the rift had become larger.

Despite the moment of happiness, I knew not all the stories had a happily ever after. Some, had yet to end.

We passed the crematorium on the way to the hospital, and my faint smile dipped to a frown. Somewhere in San Francisco, a witch roamed. The story aura still compelled Blair Danes to kidnap my husband and his sister. Like the wolf, she was aware of who she'd become. While the wolf had tried to end *Little Red Riding Hood* faster than the Keeper of Stories to remain immortal, the witch might try to twist her tale—*of course*, she'd try to twist her tale. Blair wanted to cook and eat Hansel and Gretel, and if I didn't stop her, she might succeed.

Was it worth removing the hood to find her faster?

I shook my head and tore my eyes from the window where passing buildings made my head spin.

I held tighter to my son and let myself enjoy a moment of bliss.

"Jack," I whispered.

He peeked at me with one eye, and I stroked my palm over his fuzzy head. A tiny smile curled his lips as spit bubbled around his mouth.

I placed my finger in his little palm, and he wrapped his hand around it. Frost spread from his fist to my finger as he squeezed.

And here I thought that with a second child, I'd know what to do. Of course, Jack was full of magic, powerful and likely unpredictable, and already so different from his big sister.

Hood or not, I had a brand new adventure ahead of me.

I woke in a cloudy, white heaven of fresh linens. The lights above me were dimmed and the faint smell of cleaning chemicals reminded me I'd been napping in the hospital. I rolled my head to the side to see a clear tub on a rolling table beside my bed. Inside, lay Jack swaddled tightly in a yellow blanket.

Frost had spread over the tub's plastic surface, out from where my son was curled.

I scooted to the side of the bed and reached over the edge of the tub. My thumb brushed against Jack's icy cheek. The frost pulled back, slowly disappearing into him at my touch. Warmth returned and a rosy shade blossomed over his chubby cheeks.

I smiled and rolled onto my back again.

Two dark figures stood over my bed. A gasp died in my throat. The men weren't there only seconds ago.

"Keeper," one of them spoke. I recognized the voice but couldn't place it in my grogginess. "Storyland is dying."

Storyland? Finally, recognition dawned.

"Jacob Grimm?" I asked and squinted at the two ghostly shapes. I noticed now, that they weren't solid bodies but apparitions that couldn't fully form in our world.

The older one cleared his throat. "And Will," he said.

Of course, the other brother needed equal attention. If I didn't already have two children of my own, I might consider the gods of the story world my responsibility. The older brother's name left me feeling prickly, though he had no relation to Detective Wilhelm.

"Did you hear him?" Will Grimm asked. "Storyland is dying, and you killed our only hope."

"I didn't—"

"Sherlock Holmes was investigating the changes to the rift. He was on the brink of a breakthrough when a bullet came through from the other side."

"No…" my voice trailed away as I understood.

"He's dead!" Jacob squealed and dramatically palmed his forehead.

"I think she realizes that now, Jake, thank you." Will shook his head.

"JACOB," Jacob shouted the correction to his name.

His brother only rolled his eyes. "Keeper, your world's fate has tangled with ours. If Storyland dies, so does your home."

"The entire world, not just your little, tiny, box of a house," Jacob clarified.

Will shot him an annoyed look and spoke through clenched teeth. "I was getting there, little brother." He returned his attention to me with a gaze intense enough for me to recoil. "Holmes was going to save us. But now, the responsibility is yours."

"Do you see my son?" I pointed to the rolling table. "I have to take care of him and—"

"Bring him with you!" Jacob said brightly. "We have prams in Storyland."

Prams? I knew it was another word for stroller but my slow, overwhelmed mind took extra time to get there.

"See you soon," Will said before they vanished.

Their presence left a chill in the dimly lit room. Bright light poured over the bed as the door swung open. A nurse marched inside to come squish my stomach back into place.

While she kneaded the area where my womb was still sore, I ruminated over the gods' words. The disembodied scream and the voice that followed it finally made sense. In the excitement of birth and exhaustion post labor, I'd forgotten about the invisible woman. She hadn't been invisible, simply out of sight, and on the other side of the veil—the hood. At least that little mystery was solved as a new problem presented itself.

Was our world truly in danger? What did Storyland's problems have to do with Earth's fate? A million questions narrowed down to one thought. That same thought turned over in my brain, stuck on loop like a broken record.

I killed Sherlock Holmes.

Epilogue

Dear Journal,

I didn't kill Sherlock Holmes. Detective Wilhelm did. I thought repeating it every day would convince me of the truth, but guilt still plagues me during the long nights of nursing Jack.

If he doesn't wake me with hungry cries, night sweats interrupt my sleep. Instead of Shere Khan or Godzilla, my nightmares are repeated images of wilted plants and the spontaneous combustion of people around me. Finally, it ends with me gasping for breath while the world bleeds oxygen.

I doubt the world's end will be as I've dreamed. The Brothers Grimm told me its death will start with stories. Whatever that means.

I guess I'll find out. Tomorrow I'm meeting Watson at the rift where he'll share Sherlock's studies. Because, apparently, saving the world is up to me. Again. And unfortunately, my babysitter canceled.

Emily Fluke

Up next is the sixth installment of Mari's adventures. Together with her children and friends, Mari will cross the veil and solve the mystery of Storyland's death! (Good thing alternate realities have prams too.)

Please consider leaving a review at your favorite place to purchase books if you enjoyed this story! Also, a share with your friends would be greatly appreciated. My quest as an author is to make others feel seen through the adventure of fiction. Please reach out to me and let me know if my stories have touched you. You, dear reader, are who this book was written for.

About the Author

Congenital Heart Defect survivor, Emily Fluke, finds joy and peace through the expression of writing. She is a firm believer that all stories need a little magic and a lot of excitement. Emily and her husband spend their free time wrangling two children and playing video games in their busy California lifestyle. Otherwise, you'll find Emily solving an escape room, running, or writing Magic the Gathering-based poetry.

To stay up to date on new releases and connect with me, visit my website at Emilyfluke.com or follow me on social media under Author Emily Fluke, or @emilyflukefairytales